THE LEGENDARY KINGDOMS OF ATTERA

Book 1 The Light Stones
Part 1

THE LEGENDARY KINGDOMS OF ATTERA BOOK SERIES

Published by Screech Owl Publishing
Taunton, MA
November 2016

All copy rights and properties both physical and intellectual of The Legendary Kingdoms of Attera book series are owned entirely by Author Brian R Hall. All rights reserved.

Hall, Brian R. | Author

Gutierrez, Catherine | Editor in Chief

Kutzer, Jonathan | Artist, Cover Art and Illustrations

Germain, Slade | Content Editor

O'Rourke, Justin | Illustration pg. 44

Hall, Alina A. | Media, Graphics, and Book Content Design Structure and Formatting

The story, all names, characters, and incidents portrayed in this book Legendary Kingdoms of Attera are fictitious. No identification with actual persons (living or deceased), places, buildings, and products is intended or should be inferred.

This is a work of fiction. Names, characters, businesses, places, events and incidents are either the products of the author's imagination or used in a fictitious manner. Any resemblance to actual persons, living or dead, or actual events is purely coincidental.

Printed in the U.S.A.

THE LEGENDARY KINGDOMS OF ATTERA

Book 1 The Light Stones

Part 1

B.R. HALL

SCREECH OWL PUBLISHING

CONTENTS

Prologue **9**

For Your Informational Needs... **11**

Chapter 1: A Trap and a Meadow **13**

Chapter 2: Shadows in the Mist **23**

Chapter 3: A Shade in the Woods **36**

Chapter 4: A Meadow, A Margahn, and an Ilbri **45**

Chapter 5: Talking Birds and Flying Snakes **50**

Chapter 6: Night Visions **61**

PROLOGUE

Nearly two thousand winters have come and gone since the Sarn Wars almost completely devastated the Eight Kingdoms of Attera. The good folk of Attera united together to defeat the Mongrel, Sarn, and Nephal armies of Ipolus the Enslaver and saved their world from falling under his tyrannical rule. For Ipolus didn't merely want to be High King over all who dwelt in Attera, but he also desired and demanded nothing short of God-like worship from every being who would have been under his merciless rule. Though his armies were crushed and fully routed, Ipolus himself escaped, and it has been said by many, that ever since his defeat, he had hidden somewhere in the Under-Realm, deep in the bowels of Attera, plotting and scheming on how he would execute his next attack, fully conquer and take revenge upon all those among the Eight Kingdoms who fought against him for their lives and freedom.

Now for many years, the Elder Assembly of Arden and the Ravenhawk Chief Council, working with King Wallenkor of Amara and the King of Kayna, have kept watch and continually fought against the evil forces actively operating in Attera, waiting for signs of Ipolus and his vengeful return.

In recent months, there had been a staggering increase in the amount of trade caravan attacks, as well as village and town raids, all along the two main commerce routes, the Eastern Spice Road and the Allowin River Road. It appeared that the attacks went far beyond the scope of regular brigands and highwaymen. Fearing the worst, King Wallenkor sent for help, commissioning every available scout and mercenary of the Eight Kingdoms into service, to discover the reason behind the sudden rise in caravan and village assaults. What was even more terrifying to the kings, rulers, and leaders of Attera were the many rumors and reports floating back to their ears, that the long dreaded hour was upon them at last: Ipolus had returned. Many out right refused to believe it, but the wise Zanari Sages and the Arden Assembly of Elders, who had kept watch and guard for generations, were growing more and more suspicious.

From King Wallenkor of Amara and King Simeon of Kayna, commission requests arrived in Ravenlodge, the home of the Ravenhawk Scout's Council of Chiefs, that offered great sums of gold and silver coins to send as many scouting squads that were available for hire and could come. In answer to the requests, from Crow Hollow came several Ravenhawk squads, each traveling to different locations in the far forests, trade routes, and towns of Kayna and Amara. To one of the most dangerous regions went the legendary Ravenhawk Chief, Joshen Reza, along with his adventuring companion Lurandor Hollintree, an Ilbri warrior-bard sage and their young Ravenhawk scouting apprentice Bren Reza. After many days of travel, they made their way across the entire Kingdom of Kayna and arrived in Southern Amara. After tracking a large group of raiding Margahns, in Stonewood forest, the three Ravenhawk scouts set a trap and waited…

Tinkmut
Badaboogs

FOR YOUR INFORMATIONAL NEEDS…

The Legendary Kingdoms of Attera book series uses the famous, well almost famous, Tinkmut's Gazetteer and Encyclopedia as an in-book glossary and reference tool. Excerpts from Tinkmut's compendium book will serve as an annotation tool to help educate and familiarize an outside, world traveler who has made his way fortunately, or hopefully not unfortunately, to Attera for the first time, and desires to know all he can about this new mystical, wondrous, glorious, fascinating… okay, you get the idea… realm. Since we hope to make your stay in Attera a long and enjoyable one, we wanted to ensure that a glossary/ encyclopedia, functioning also as a directional map, is easily accessible, helping all new travelers in Attera explore this vast and multifaceted realm without getting lost and frustrated.

The legendary scholar sage and woodland gnome, Robnob Haborav started working on a universal gazetteer and encyclopedia to benefit and educate the travelers, adventurers, and curious folk of Attera. He moved on to other projects and handed the book down to his nephew and apprentice Tinkmut Badaboogs to finish, complete or just add to it at least. Robnob told Tinkmut, who was easily made happy and content over the smallest of things, that if he took on the responsibility of diligently working on adding to the books as he experienced new people, places, monsters, plants, and so forth, that he could place his name on the book. Tinkmut became so happy at this. That overboard feeling of joy turned into a full blown obsession, as he seemed to always be adding things into it, and when he wasn't working on it, he was talking about it more than most of his close friends could possibly hope to tolerate. At times, well, again to be honest, most of the time, Robnob wondered whether or not he regretted giving Tinkmut the job which had appeared to encourage Tinkmut to never ever seem to run out of words talking about it. This soon annoyed Robnob, and most of Arden who knew him closely, or the strangers who bumped into him and regrettably asked him about his book and what he was writing in it; "annoyance without end" as Robnob would say. My last epiphany of honesty: the real truth was what annoyed Robnob the most, was that when someone else talked all the time, it lessened the amount of time that he had opportunity to talk, which he loved to do so himself as much as his long winded, fast speaking nephew. So when reading the recorded historical accounts of The Legendary Kingdoms of Attera, make sure you read Tinkmut's excerpts and never forget the sacrifices of Robnob and Tinkmut, and what they endured (and everyone else around them), to make the largest, most comprehensive and accurate gazetteer to be found anywhere in the Eight Kingdoms.

Robnob Haborav

Chapter 1

A TRAP AND A MEADOW

The morning sun began to break over the horizon. Rays of the early dawn slowly started to penetrate through the shadows of the surrounding forest. A cloud of mist, mildly reflecting the glowing light, crept slowly across the meadow with the likeness of a rogue cloud. Bren welcomed the dim visibility the breaking light was giving him, along with its warmth. He had lain in a thicket of dense brush since late in the evening yesterday. The nighttime air brought with it moisture that blanketed him and the surrounding shrubbery with a heavy dew. He felt soaked to the bone which made his body ache and stiffen up. He mildly shook with the chills, on and off through most of the hours of darkness, as the twin moons Sa-lu-yan and Sama-yin chased one another across the star-filled sky. Needless to say, he spent the night feeling slightly irritated and "contently annoyed" as Robnob the Gnome used to say to describe certain pesky but necessary situations that life puts us through.

The chaotic chattering music of various recognizable and unrecognizable insects seemed to perform their orchestra nonstop all night. They were tireless and relentless in their late hour song making. Bren wondered how these nightly noise makers could go all night chattering without the need for any breaks or rest. The nippy damp air, combined with the nightly noises, stole all chances he might have had for any type of reasonable rest. He would have been happy if he was at least comfortable enough to reflect on his duties of the mission he was there on. His mentors Joshen and Lurandor gave him a strategic role to carry out. They had carefully laid out the plans for a trap. This was his first Ravenhawk* mission and the first time he had ever traveled to the Stonewood Forest or been this far from home. All this added to the pressure he felt to not fail to do his part exactly as it was precisely laid out. Bren, who was orphaned at the age of two, grew up in the household of the gnome and scholar sage, Robnob Haborav and his wife Reyva. Robnob Haborav was a very eccentric, if not a strangely mysterious, sort of fellow. Many in the gnome and surrounding communities would say he was odd and peculiar, but that he was so, in a jolly, good sort of way. He spent most of his time researching and developing all sorts of inventions. Some of his creations were quite genius and useful while others were never fully completed and therefore useless; most of which were of the latter. Robnob and Reyva were great, loving caretakers for Bren. Nonetheless, most Mejian children had good Mejian parents to raise them, train and educate them in the ancient ways of the Mejian people. The

---

Tinkmut's Gazetteer and Encyclopedia of Attera

WORKING CLASSES OF ATTERA

Excerpt, Added and Written by Robnob Haborav - Woodland Gnome and Scholar Sage

THE RAVENHAWKS—Founded and formed by Mejian scouts and warriors after the Sarn Wars nearly two thousand winters ago. The Ravenhawks are lead and governed by Eight Elder Chiefs (each from one of the Eight Tribes of Mejia). The Ravenhawks are best described as a professional scouting and body guard for hire agency. They are often commissioned to escort and protect trade caravans or royal entourages traveling between towns or kingdoms. They are often hired by villages as well to deal with various monsters or evil creatures that are too difficult to exterminate or deal with. They are mostly made up of native Mejian people but over time allowed other folk and races into their ranks. They are considered to be the most skilled scouts, warriors, and hunters of all the Eight Kingdoms of Attera. They also serve as the main elite fighting force for the people and Kingdom of Mejia.

Tinkmut's Gazetteer and Encyclopedia of Attera

THE KINGDOMS, TOWNS, AND VILLAGES OF ATTERA

Excerpt, added and written by Robnob Haborav - Woodland Gnome and Scholar Sage

THE KINGDOM OF MEJIA—Mejia, one of the Eight Kingdoms of Attera, is located with the Kingdom of Arden to its North and West sides and the Kingdom of Kardinia to its South. The entire Kingdom of Mejia lies in a vast valley in the middle of the Erez Mountain range. Mejia was established and named after Leban Mejia. Traveling north up the Arden River, Leban Mejia passed through a gap in the southern Erez Mountains and with his eight sons and their families, came into a land of hills, steppes and plains surrounded by tall, steep mountains. Each son claimed an area of land and named it after himself. This was how the eight provinces and tribes of Mejia were formed. The Mejian people are known for their distinctive olive skin and dark wavy hair. The Province of Zakreeya is the recognized capital of Mejia. A thousand years after Leban and his families established Mejia as their homeland, Mejia was nearly devastated by the Sarn Wars as well as the rest of the Kingdoms of Attera. As a result, a large portion of the tribes left Mejia and lived as nomads traveling between the Kingdoms of Attera. Many travel in small caravans of wagons between villages and towns performing shows as singers, dancers and skilled entertainers. In the Province of Zakreeya resides the largest remnant population of Mejia. The largest population of Mejians outside of the Kingdom of Mejia lives in Crow Hollow, located in the Greentree Mountains, in the northern parts of the Kingdom of Arden. There in Crow Hollow at a place called Ravenlodge was established the home of the Ravenhawks' Elder Chief Council. The Mejians are most famous for their creation of the Ravenhawk Scouts, their traveling performing entertainment shows, and their part in fighting against the evil of Ipolus' armies during the Sarn Wars. They are considered by many to be the best warriors and scouts among all the folk of Attera.

folk of Mejia* were very clan and family-oriented. Their rich culture and heritage had been what had kept their people together and alive after many generations of most of the tribes living nomadically throughout various parts of Attera. Bren was treated poorly among children of his peer group since they all, for the most part, saw him as less of a fellow Mejian and more like a foreign outcast. All they focused on about Bren was the fact that he lived in a gnomish tree home and had two gnomes for adopted parents. Children can be mean and cruel, and Bren found this out the hard way, as he was often teased and called many unsavory nicknames. The worst thing is that almost none of the Mejian children his age wanted his friendship and sadly, most wanted nothing to do with him at all. Bren was very intelligent and very wise, well beyond what someone his age should normally be. Robnob had, on more than one occasion when talking to other sages and scholars, stated that there was something peculiarly different about Bren in the way he saw and understood the world around him.

"That child is brilliantly good at being a uniquely odd but genius thinker," Robnob would say to his wife Reyva, nearly every time Bren said or did something that reflected his "brilliantly odd way of thinking." The young Mejian's distinctively brilliant thoughts, words and actions often left Robnob and Reyva shaking their heads in awe, and sometimes, just shaking their heads in curious confusion.

Lurandor the Ilbri, when discussing his observations about Bren with Joshen, had many times in the past said that the young Mejian was an "old mind and spirit dwelling in a young body." All of Bren's caretakers and mentors had concluded unanimously that there was something different but very special about Bren. He was an anomaly and an enigma who they knew they didn't completely comprehend. They all knew fated providence had intentionally born him at this time, in this age of Attera, for a purpose that no one yet fully or even partially understood. One thing was for certain; Bren would impact the world around him in a large way when his time came to catch up with his destiny.

Sadly though, it is an unfortunate truth, and part of life, that most gifted children like Bren, because of their intellectual and special internal ways of seeing the world, are often singled out and shunned by their peer group since they don't usually fit into the norm. Bren never realized his enjoying hanging out with adults much more than children his own age was due to his extremely high level of intelligence. He had always just felt like he was weird and strange and that was the reason he was so distant from his peers. Bren was lonely, needless to say, and always seemed and felt out of place and awkward around other children of Mejia and Arden. Only Kellan Reza, who was a few winters older than Bren and also from Bren's clan, the Reza Turtle Clan, had treated him as a real friend should and at times like a younger brother. Kellan Reza was strong and skillful, and nearly all the Mejians living in Crow Hollow would agree and often speak about how one day he would be a powerful warrior among the Mejian Ravenhawks and a mighty Ravenhawk Chieftain. There was much talk and speculation around the campfires and hearths of Crow Hollow and parts of Arden that Kellan Reza would one day be as legendary as Joshen himself. Whenever he was around, no one would dare pick on or call Bren childishly taunting names. Bren looked up to Kellan as an older brother and a role model. There were few folk left of the Reza clan, and the remaining clan members stuck together as a tight family.

    Tinkmut Boogs, a young gnome who was a nephew of Robnob, was Bren's best friend. Tinkmut himself was, as some would put it and they often did of course, quite "colorful" in his personality, being both eccentric and unique and in some ways, comical in his mannerisms and speech. It goes without saying that having the flamboyant and sometimes over-talkative Tinkmut Boogs as a best friend didn't do much to help Bren's rapport with the other Ravenhawk children his age. Their close friendship sometimes added fuel to the fire and fanned the flames that kept the young boy drawing the wrong kind of attention to himself among his Mejian peer circle.

    Bren recently had to deal with a very personal and painful failure that was amplified by what he perceived as a complete public humiliation. Just over a couple of months ago, Bren took his Ravenhawk rank test to go to the next scout level. He felt he had to do well and excel far above the other participants to prove to his Mejian peers that he was as good as they and that he belonged among their ranks and in their social groups. By thinking this way, Bren placed a great weight of heaviness and burden on his mind and heart giving himself anxiety and worry over the challenge of meeting his own contrived expectations. This was more pressure and stress than almost any single child his age could bear. He also felt he had to perform flawlessly during the tests because he had Joshen as a mentor. Joshen was a legend among the Ravenhawks and was a famous hero-like figure whose exploits had reached near myth status among the folk of Attera. Having trained under Joshen, Bren knew that expectations from everyone were that he would excel and pass the tests with a great performance and win many honors. Ravenhawks naturally reasoned that Bren, having Joshen as a mentor, had no excuses to not do well at any of the Scout Ranks trials. Bren knew the honor and prestige of Joshen's name was carried on his back, or at least he perceived it to be that way. The Reza clan had diminished over the years under strange unexplained circumstances. During the last rank advancement trials, Bren was the only one out of hundreds of participants to represent the Reza Mejian Clan of the Turtle. This was just another factor among many that also added weight to the pressure he was putting on himself. Weeks of stress, anxiety, and obsessive worry went by,

Tinkmut's Gazetteer and Encyclopedia of Attera

WORKING CLASSES OF ATTERA

Excerpt, added and written by Robnob Haborav - Woodland Gnome and Scholar Sage

THE RAVENHAWKS RANKS AND LEADERSHIP – There are seven rank levels in the Ravenhawk Scouts. Each one wears a different knit hat that is used to identify rank. All testing trials are overseen and judged by the Ravenhawk Grand Council of Chieftains.

1. **Finch Scout** (Novice Scout): White stripe hat. Person is a beginner and immediately starts being mentored in the scouting arts. Learning: tracking, combat arts, hunting and many more skills needed to become a professional Ravenhawk.

2. **Sparrow Hawk Scout** (Apprentice Scout): Green stripe hat. Person passes the trials of the novice and is assigned to be trained under a Master Scout. At this time, they are allowed to go on commissioned missions with their master scout.

3. **Crow Scout** (Veteran Scout): Brown stripe hat. Completed the scout trials. Now a Crow Scout is a professional scout but still must remain under a Master Scout until their tutelage is complete. They may test for the Master Scout level once the Master Scout they are under decides they are ready.

4. **Falcon Scout** (Master Scout): Blue stripe hat. Once the trials have been passed a professional veteran scout may then be called a Master Scout.

5. **Condor Scout** (Captain Scout): Red stripe hat. If the person passes the trials, this scout can become a Captain and then may lead a scout squad or take on apprentices.

6. **Nighthawk Scout** (Chieftain Scout): Black stripe on hat. This scout is chosen by the Ravenhawk Council from the master scouts to be a chief. A chief is an overseer of a region of Attera or over a group of master scouts.

7. **Elder Owl Scout** (A master scout and warrior): Red and black stripe on hat. May become part of the Ravenhawk Grand Council of Chieftains. The judges over the council are made up of 8 Ravenhawk chiefs, one from each tribe of Mejia so that all the tribes are represented equally.

along with many sleepless nights, for Bren. All this turmoil just grew and welled up inside Bren that by the time the trials came, Bren was a mental and nervous wreck. The inevitable of course happened during the trials. His anxiety and shaky nerves took over causing him to fail all parts of the trials miserably. How many children his age could have handled so much without falling completely apart? He was now ashamed to even show himself in Crow Hollow or anywhere else where other Ravenhawks or Mejians gathered.

Failing the Ravenhawk ranking trials was devastating for Bren to say the least; it created deep, emotional scars that would be with Bren for life. He still held the rank of Finch Scout, the novice rank level of the Ravenhawk scouts. If he had passed, he would have gone to the next level and become a Sparrow Hawk, which is an intermediate level scout. This gnawed at Bren and his mind had now often obsessed over replaying and dwelling on vivid memories of his failure to pass the trials. He felt as if he let down his mentors Joshen and Lurandor, as well as Robnob the Gnome. He imagined and thought that he not only failed, but that he had done so in an epically poor and embarrassing manner. Bren, as most anybody of high intelligence does, kept analyzing in his mind what happened, causing him, as a result, to experience a constant flow of shame and guilt-ridden feelings. Both of these devastating emotional forces worked and grew in him, eating away at his heart, warping his self-image and gradually stealing all his self-confidence and self-worth. Every piece of wisdom has its price. If we don't learn from our pain then our scars only make us ugly and fail to serve as reminders visually guiding our paths forward.

Only someone who has the rank of a Sparrow Hawk* Scout by order of the Ravenhawk Council of Chieftains is allowed to go on full commissioned missions. Joshen Reza, who was a Master Chief, often didn't work by the rules and made Bren the exception to the rule. He brought the young Mejian on a mission commissioned by King Vilkahm Wallenkor, the High King of Amara, to rid the Allowin River trade road of bandits, thieves and Margahn raiding parties. Bren should have understood this meant that Joshen and Lurandor had great faith in him by bringing him along, hundreds of miles from his home in Cedar Ridge Hollow. Sadly he was too upset and self-absorbed reminiscing in pain about his poor performance at the trials to clearly see that his mentors hadn't lost a shred of faith in him. By taking him on the current mission, Joshen and Lurandor, as well as Robnob, thought it would do him some good to get away from his recent bad experiences and get him focused on something else as he healed from his inner wounds. All three agreed that though he was in the state that he was in, he was more than ready for his first full Ravenhawk mission.

As Bren currently now lay in his position with all of these factors at work inside him, he struggled to keep his thoughts bound together. He put forth great effort to keep his mind in a state of deep meditative concentration. With circumstances as they were, he found himself, for most part of the night, in an uncomfortable groggy state, dozing and fighting to stay out of the realm of dreams and bad memories from the past. He knew he needed to focus on the next day's plans. Bren had high expectations (mostly unrealistic) for his first Ravenhawk mission. So far this was nothing like what he had anticipated. He was so afraid he would fail again; only this time, life and death consequences were in the mix.

"The books in Robnob's library never told any story about the fabled heroes of Attera's ancient past lying in the weeds soaked with dew all night feeling 'comfortably miserable,'" Bren thought, another somewhat used term he had heard more times than he cared to count.

"Comfortably miserable" was a phrase he often heard Robnob say from time to time. Bren thought now he understood that phrase with realistic clarity.

"So much for high adventure. I guess this is all necessary to endure as a hero strives down the path to glory and honor," thought Bren. He clearly understood the honor of their mission, but under the current circumstances, he was troubled to find the glory in it or at least the type of glory his young, ideologically naive mind understood it to be. He wrapped his Ravenhawk scout cloak tighter around him and pulled the hood of it slightly back to where he could see his surroundings a little better. He adjusted the brooch on the cowl of his cloak. The brooch he had on was like the one his mentor wore. It was made of a bronze looking metal and was in the shape of a turtle. This unique turtle emblem was the symbol of his tribe. All the Mejians who were descendants of Reza used the turtle as their emblem of identity.

Though he was weary and tired from a restless night lying exposed to the elements in his position, Bren knew there was no room for mistakes and was able to keep his head about him as he made sure to make every one of his movements as smooth and steady as possible, just as Joshen had taught him.

"Jerky unnatural movements draw unwanted visual attention when you attempt to hide and camouflage yourself against the background of a natural setting. You must move, feel and think natural. You must become a part of where you're seeking to conceal yourself to properly blend in. To successfully hide in an environment, you must become the environment. When you break these precepts, you will surely reveal your position to an enemy. You might as well stand up and wave them over for dinner." The voice of Joshen spoke in his head as Bren remembered one of his teachings that he now applied to his current circumstance.

He had heard that phrase or something like it more times than he cared to imagine.

His multi-colored, earthen-schemed cloak, the traditional cloak of a Ravenhawk scout, seemed to blend into any outdoor environment. Its natural forest-shape pattern faded its wearer to visually disappear among both tree and leaf. This now made him virtually invisible. Where he was lying in his current position was a place chosen for the best camouflage he could find. He was lying out on his stomach in a patch of dense brush that was almost shoulder high to the average man. As long as he stayed still and moved slowly, he would be virtually unseen and undetectable to any wandering eyes. He carefully remained aware of the fact though that one quick movement would be all it would take to alert any enemy or preying monster scouting the area.

"Think natural and you will be natural. Then you will not just be trying to hide in your surrounding environment but you become a part of it, fading into the scenery." The young Ravenhawk scout again remembered Joshen's teachings as his memories played them out in his mind.

"It's hard to think or feel natural when there seems to be something unnatural that I sense and feel in the air," thought Bren to himself. Part of him, that he was trying to keep suppressed, wished he was wrapped in his wool blanket in his cozy bed at home rather than being wrapped in a scout cloak, lying in rough feeling brush all night.

As the morning sun began to make its full appearance over the horizon, he felt something stir his spirit that fully woke him up and sobered his mind. Tesha, the second sun hued with blue, and Asha, the third sun which glowed in the color of red, had not broken above the horizon yet. Each day, the two smaller orbs chased Mesham, the much larger, brighter golden sun across the sky of Attera. It wasn't the sun rays and their warmth that had brought Bren to an alert state; it was a tinge of stirred uneasiness that suddenly swept over him like a murky blanket. This invasive feeling shook him and woke him up with similar effectiveness as the appetizing fragrances coming from Reyva's cooking each morning would reach his room located at the top of Robnob's tree home and wake him.

The warm light of dawn should have brought comfort but now he felt something was out of place. Ravenhawks are not trained to just survive on their physical senses but to be attuned, connecting with their surroundings with their feelings. And at this moment, he felt a disturbance in his gut. His spiritual discernment was nagging at his young mind. He knew he had to risk moving to get a more panoramic view. Bren had noticed the first rays of the golden morning sun had brought with it the sound of song birds, bringing life to the forest and the surrounding meadow with their melodies and chatter. The songs were everywhere except for the far eastern side of the woods. The young Mejian Ravenhawk took note of this in his mind.

A few moments before, he could smell the fresh morning dew coming from the flowers scented with early spring pollen.

"All I smell now is something out of place and sour carried in the morning breeze mixed with the various common natural forest odors," he thought to himself.

Joshen had trained him well, giving him the ability to use all of his senses that he developed during training. He was taught to decipher any clues his environment may reveal, keeping him aware of any possible threats before they are in range close enough to be dangerous to him. Despite his age of twelve winters, he had a firm grasp on wood craft skills far beyond most his physical maturity level. This was mostly due to the expert teachings of Joshen who was well known throughout most of Attera as one of the most skilled and formidable Ravenhawk scouts alive. Though Joshen, a Master Chief rank scout, refused to be a part of the Ravenhawk chief council, the Ravenhawk scouts hardly made any decisions without involving him in some way, whether he desired to be involved or not.

Bren looked to the eastern side of the meadow again and eyed the fog as it crept ominously out of the forest. It was thick and looked as if it were a great cloud from the sky that had come down to roam above the surface, flowing close over the ground.

He then peered down from the small cliff he was hiding on to the fake camp site below. The fire burned low and the tent ruffled slightly in the morning breeze. It comforted Bren somewhat in knowing Joshen and Lurandor had been so methodical and precise in laying out the plans for their trap.

His position was located on top of a small cliff wall that overlooked the meadow and camp some fifteen feet below. Forty paces or so on the left hand side of the camp (Bren's left side facing the camp), there stood among the high field grass some tall stone pillars about ten feet high and six feet thick. Parts of them were crumbling and most were covered with moss and vines. The pillars had seen countless years of erosion and no one, not even the local sages or bards, knew the tale of their origin. They were the remnant of some lost, ancient civilization. Their purpose was forgotten long ago, lost in antiquity. The Stonewood Forest was full of the large obelisk-like stone structures. They seemed to be randomly spread throughout the forest with no apparent reason or order. Two of these strange pillars stood near the northwest side of the makeshift camp. On top of these pillars, invisible to human eyes, sat the living legend of Attera himself, Joshen, son of Reza, a Mejian, a descendant of Leban, like Bren. Beside him sat Lurandor the Ilbri. Covered in their scout cloaks, they seemed to be a part of the ancient stone, blending in with the hue of the pillar. They looked like they were a perforation of the stone instead of separate shapes sitting on them. Even a few birds flying in the morning breeze almost landed on each of them several times, thinking they were a part of the stones. Like Bren, Joshen and Lurandor stayed awake most of the night sitting atop of the pillars and were stiff and sore from holding their camouflaged positions the entire time. Now they were all on keen alert and waiting for their prey to fall into the trap.

Joshen lifted his hand slowly. Anyone seeing this, not knowing he was there, would have been greatly startled and sworn that a portion of the rock was coming alive. The movement was a risky one but Joshen deemed it necessary. Joshen's hand proceeded to make small tight patterns in the air. These were the secret hand language the Mejian scouts used to communicate in silence so as not to make any sounds that could alert or draw unwanted attention. They called it "hand whispering." This hand language was only known to the Mejians and the Ilbri who taught it to them. Bren, who had learned the language from Joshen, was still a novice but could decipher it with some proficiency. "The fog, the mist… get ready… they are coming with a jingrol," was what Bren read from Joshen's hand whispering language.

Joshen then hid his hand back concealing it underneath the cover of his cloak and again became visually part of the stone he sat upon. Bren didn't need to respond. He knew the "they" Joshen was referring to were the mongrel race, the Margahns, created and bred by the Evil One Ipolus. The Margahns were created by Ipolus many ages ago by wickedly doing what was forbidden by Ya-El the all-Creator. He mixed the seed and flesh of man with pigs, coyotes, hyenas and apes. The Margahns were a walking blasphemy to the All-Creator Ya-el. The vile race had coal black and brown patched fur and skin with piggish, canine faces and fanged teeth. They are a wicked sort of creature often called "goblins" by some of the speaking races throughout the Eight Kingdoms. Much evil has been

Margahns

done in Attera by their hands since the time they walked out of Ipolus's dark pits and plagued the lands of Sarnia.

The Margahn war pack had brought with them the jingrol, a large hairy beast that was also another of Ipolus's hybrid-bred mongrels. A jingrol was usually the size of a large elephant. They have a mouth full of sharp horn-like teeth, large enough to swallow two grown men at once and a cow if it desired. Great ivory horns shaped like those of a mountain ram rose from the crown of their heads to form half crescent shapes. Many sturdy stone walls had crumbled from the charging impact of those horns that rested on the head of the enormous beasts. Their bodies were covered with dense multicolored fur (mostly red and brown colored) that bushed out all over their head and torso and streamed downward in patches like the branches of a great willow tree. They traveled on all fours but can stand on two legs at times when the need arises. Jingrols were larger than mountain giants, and being both dangerous in strength and aggressive in temperament, they were feared by even some of the most stout-of-heart warriors in Attera. The hostile creatures were strong enough to rip a tree from its roots with their clawed hands without much strain of effort.

Bren held his position and looked through the brush toward the fog. He nervously smiled to himself as he had figured out the enemy's direction and sensed their looming presence before Joshen could warn him. He felt a small sense of satisfaction in this. His smile did not last long though. He began to become tense with fear and anxiety. After all, at twelve, this was Bren's first time fighting in a real skirmish.

"Anticipating danger in the mind often leads to more fear than needed in the heart," Bren remembered Robnob the Gnome used to say this a lot. This did little to comfort Bren's foreboding feeling now. Reality was setting in. He realized they were in for a real battle that was unlike any he imagined in his head or read in a book. He learned quickly reality had a completely different feel to it; one he found that he didn't all together like at the moment.

Even though strategically placed in a safe position chosen by Joshen, Bren still didn't feel very safe. He felt familiar hands of anxiety gripping him again just as what laid its hands on him during the Ravenhawk Scout trials. He knew he had to get back a hold of himself. He took a slow deep breath counting to four as he inhaled and four as he exhaled, just like Joshen had taught him. After he took several methodical breaths this way, he felt his heart rate slow down again and he began to feel calm once more; as calm as anyone could expect to feel in his unique set of circumstances. Even though Joshen had purpose-

A Jingrol

ly positioned him atop the twelve foot cliff overlooking the fake camp to keep him safely out of the way during the fight to come, Bren was still feeling quite nervous. His focus on the breathing techniques that the Ravenhawks regularly used helped keep him in control over the quaking feeling in his stomach caused by his nerves.

The young Ravenhawk looked once more toward his camouflaged companions, gaining strength from the knowledge that he was with two living legends whose exploits were told in every tavern across the woodland areas of Arden and Kayna. Bren couldn't help but feel he was a burden and nothing more to his skilled companions. Silently he hoped he could contribute and do his part. He didn't want his companions to be distracted from their purpose by being too overly protective of him. This was Bren's first true Ravenhawk mission, and in his mind he had a lot of undue pressure that he had put there himself, same as he had months earlier when he faced the ranking trials.

Bren looked down at the camp seeing the large tent. From there his eyes went to the leaf-filled, body-shaped sleeping blankets around a fire that was slowly roasting meats hung over it. It was this alluring odor that was drawing their bait out and into their trap. Bren's gaze looked across the high grasses of the meadow. More stone pillars appeared visibly in the early morning light as the sun rays revealed more and more of what was hidden in the dark of night. The ancient monolith pillars that stood scattered in random patterns across the meadow were now becoming more visible. Bren's eyes had played tricks on him all night; he had imagined the stones coming to life as large giants that started moving slowly and menacingly towards him. Now in the dim light of dawn, he decided and was thankful that they looked a lot less menacing. Looking closely at the mysterious stones, he wondered who or what had made them and for what purpose.

Now these ancient pillars seemed like small mountains among the clouds as the rolling fog moved from the forest and crept across the meadow. Slowly, the dense fog moved with the push of a warm spring breeze. It blanketed the meadow, swallowing each pillar as it moved forward. Bren stared at the misty morning fog trying to peer past its encompassing veil. He found that he couldn't see through it. As it inched its way closer, Bren had to strain to keep his fear swallowed down. Each inch forward seemed like an eternity. The young Ravenhawk scout knew all too soon, the fog would be bringing with it hidden danger coming upon their positions all too quickly. Bren wished the wind would change directions and blow the cloud of fog back into the forest and take its hidden dangers with it.

Chapter 2

SHADOWS IN THE MIST

Soon the meadow became much too quiet as the thick foggy mist overtook the last pillar of the meadow before it reached the camp. Bren could feel his heartbeat pounding in his stomach as the morning cloud covered the camp, the stone pillars and the cliff where he and his companions were positioned. He could feel the dampness and the nearness of something wicked lurking in the veil of mist that was now shrouding the entire meadow in darkness. He lay quietly in anticipation as he felt the chill as a result of the fog that was dimming the rays of the morning dawn. Bren scanned the area using the full extent and limitations of his eyes as he looked through the blanket of mist. Through the grayness, he could still see the camp and the pillars where his two companions were waiting. The mist didn't totally limit his sight as he discovered that he could still see a short distance in the fog as it covered everything around him.

    Bren's heart skipped and his stomach shook as he saw dark shapes that were hunched over, making their way towards the camp. There seemed to be many of them as they moved slowly and steadily, spread out in jagged formations. Soon they got closer and closer and he could make out their ape-like movements as they tried to move as stealthily as possible through the tall meadow grass. Bren knew without a shadow of doubt they were Margahns, the same ones who had probably been attacking farms and caravans in the forest along the Allowin River. He had never seen one alive before this day but had heard enough stories of the wicked creatures to know one when he saw it. They crept slowly with crooked swords and spiked clubs drawn, while those that had them got their crude spears ready as they moved forward. Joshen had planned on maybe a few dozen, a small war party, but the moving creeping shapes coming across the meadow now seemed at least twice that number, if not more.

"This is not at all by any calculations looking good," thought Bren.

He blinked his eyes to clear them out and looked into the misty meadow below. He couldn't believe his eyes and what they saw. One of the pillars appeared to be moving with them. It seemed as if his imagined terrors from last night were coming true, as something sinister, from what he thought was previously only confined to his imagination, was now coming to life.

"Wait!" The small voice in Bren's conscious rational thought spoke.

"I know what that is! It's a jingrol!" Bren remembered Joshen had warned him earlier about it while hand whispering to him. The Margahns often brought jingrols with them as back up when they went on raiding parties. This group was more than likely returning to their mountain lairs after two nights of attacking and ransacking hunters and nearby forest villages and farms. This mongrel war party, with its fourteen-foot tall jingrol, could have easily slaughtered an entire caravan with armed bodyguards. To Bren it seemed that things were not only looking bad but were starting to look downright dreadful.

Just as the attacking creatures neared the camp, things got even worse as something unexpected happened that their carefully laid out trap didn't count on or factor in. Bren was preparing to do his part in the planned out trap. His function was to simply throw the impact bombs which were created by Nob. The impact bombs were in the shape of walnut sized gray orbs. The balls which explode when thrown against the ground create a blast big enough to kill or knock out a small group of foes. The plan was that the bomb explosions would cause enough madness and confusion and kill many in the ranks of the attacking Margahns that they wouldn't notice the barrage of deadly arrow strikes reigning down on them from Joshen and Lurandor until it was too late.

As the Margahns drew close to the camp, Bren's heart raced again. Inside his cloak, his right hand was caressing the pouch which held the impact bombs Nob had made. He was running through the plan in his head once again.

"The moment the Margahns enter the camp, I cannot hesitate… I must throw as many impact bombs as I can… I need to stay focused and do my part which is crucial to set up and spring into motion the rest of planned out trap." The young Mejian nervously told himself silently.

Bren recalled the well laid out plans, running through them in his mind over and over. This helped him get his attention on what needed to be done and off of dwelling on being nervous and all the things that could go wrong, or more accurately, all the things he could do wrong.

He also remembered he needed to squeeze each one for a second in his hand to activate the bombs and then throw them. Robnob had told him if he forgot this, the impact bombs he threw would not explode. Bren took a few mental notes to remember this.

Soberly once again, Bren reminded himself that the diversion of the bombs exploding was the initial key, crucial to unlocking the next sequence of steps to set in motion the entire desired plan of their precisely laid out trap.

Bren's heart rate sped up as he was about to launch his bomb attack as the first Margahn came near the camp. Just as he tensed to spring up, he heard a noise in the thick brush from somewhere behind him. This noise was alarmingly out of place against the usual forest sounds he had been hearing all night and through the early morning. His heart froze in his chest as he realized something was crawling in the brush behind him. By the sound he was hearing, Bren knew it wasn't an animal.

"It also wasn't a Margahn. I would have already smelled it," he thought to himself.

Thrown into a whirlwind of possibilities that his mind instantly contrived, Bren simply didn't know what to do.

"Should I continue with the plan?" He asked himself. "Is something crawling toward me to attack me?"

A flood of questions similar to these entered and filled his young mind.

"What terrible creature from the forest is creeping towards me I wonder?" Thought Bren as he imagined some horrid monster crawling closer and closer to him, catching him by the feet, and dragging him off into the darkness of the woods. He then realized he had to keep his overactive imagination at bay for the time being and deal with the reality of what was happening.

"If I turn to face it, whatever 'it' may happen to be without throwing my impact bombs at the Margahns, I will have then given away my position and have horribly ruined the plan." Bren quickly marked that idea as a wrong choice.

"I can't fail Joshen and Lurandor," spoke his heart to his mind.

Many similar thoughts swirled through his panicking mind as leaves would blow about in a storm. He almost cried for the first time in a long time. He felt frustrated, angry and even worse, the icy fingers of despair begin to grip and chill his heart.

"If I lay here, whatever is coming from behind me will have me for sure if it knows I'm here or even by chance it crawls upon me and finds me unintentionally in the tall grass and bushes. Either way I'm caught!" Bren deliberated.

"If I stand, it will know I'm here, but I need to throw the bombs any second now," thought Bren, realizing he was running out of 'ifs' and that meant he was running out of possible options that he could contrive up being in such a situation as he was.

"I'm caught between the hammer and anvil, as Robnob used to say," thought Bren.

"The best swords in the world spent a long time being forged between the hammer and anvil. It is here where the strength of the blade is forged and beaten into the desired shape of the smith." He heard the words of his mentor Joshen echoing in his head.

For a brief moment, he wondered if Ya-El's mighty hammer was working on him, pounding him and causing change in the fibers of his being. The situation now demanded him to be decisive one way or another. He had to make a choice and deciding to do nothing was still making a major choice.

"What do I do? I need help but no one can help me," he thought, almost losing a tear.

"Be still, and trust." Bren heard a small voice in his head. He heard it so clearly that it almost seemed audible. So Bren did what he heard and just laid still. He wasn't a child of much faith or trust. He had to keep pushing memories of his recent past failures out of his head that were birthing doubt in him. Throughout his young life he always had trouble with putting his trust in worldly or otherworldly things. Now he realized in this moment, he would have to muster up at least a small amount of faith before he could choose to do anything. This voice he heard seemed not to be his own nor did it seem to be an echo from a recollection of a distant memory. Something about this voice, though he knew not from whence it came, sounded safe and familiar to him.

Eventually he mustered enough courage that was just barely the size of a grain of salt in his heart. It gave him enough strength. Was it enough so he could trust in the voice that he heard? At this moment, as hopelessness set in, he realized it was all he had.

Bren heard the crawling from behind clearer as it got closer and closer, inching near him.

"Be still and trust." He heard again. A voice that came from the outside or one that came from somewhere deep inside him echoed once more traveling straight to his heart. He really wasn't sure what was happening to him. He was in such a state of panic that he felt as if he could hardly stay still for any amount of time. He just wanted to flee but something held him in place. Bren, looking back later, would remember that he felt like a large hand held him in place. It was an indescribable feeling being in one of those events in your life that you just can't put into words, but you can never forget the nostalgic sensation you got every time it came to your memory.

The crawling became two distinct sounds. Bren now discerned there were two things moving near him. The two separate moving sounds made their way to rest beside him on both his flanks parallel to the cliff's edge. There, the two unknown crawling entities became still and eerily silent; they were obviously at the end of their destination. Bren roughly estimated that they had to be at least a three-foot distance from him on either side. He realized that they seemed not to have detected him. He dared not move or they would have easily discovered him. The thick brush and his camouflaged Ravenhawk scout cloak had hidden him well, saving his life.

The sounds they had made crawling to rest beside his position revealed two things to Bren. First, they are definitely human. Second, they were very skilled in stealth and woodcraft. In his heart he knew they were dangerous. Something else that troubled him more; he sensed an aura from them that was permeated with power and darkness that drove fear in Bren's perceptive heart. Even though he was in a state of near-crippling panic and terror, he was still able to focus enough to assess the overall situation. Painfully he now felt the same as he did when his nerves went into a frenzy and his bodily controls locked up causing him to fail his scout rank testing trials.

Bren's skill at detecting the nature of sounds was very keen, thanks again to the skillful teaching of his mentor and his diligent training. That is what kept him from completely freezing up and ceasing functioning with his learned scouting skill abilities.

The mysteriously veiled figure to his left started making movement sounds. The movements that Bren heard were smooth and calculated. Bren concluded by analyzing the actions from the sounds that whoever or whatever was next to him made movements that only a professional, someone highly skilled in his craft, could make.

"Well I guess it's a very slim chance these two are here to shake hands and make new friendly acquaintances," Bren mused, surprised that he was able to keep a touch of humor in his thoughts while in such a dire and perilously, volatile situation.

"No, without a single doubt they are dangerous and their intent is for evil. Of all the countless safer places in the Eight Kingdoms of Attera I could be right now, and well, here I am," Bren thought to himself.

Bren took that opportunity to use the stranger's movement sounds to mask the noises he himself made moving so that neither of the two darkly shrouded figures on each of his flanks would hear him as he pulled his cloak hood back and turned to take a peek at his unforeseen and certainly unwelcome visitors. Bren looked through a small breach in the high brush and weeds. What he saw instantly disturbed him greatly. A man in all black with a hood and mask that only left his eyes uncovered was crouching in the high brush. He had a black bow in his hand. He was holding it steady and vertical. Bren knew this was a camouflaging stealth tactic used to blend the bow with the vertical pattern of the surrounding weeds and brush.

"This wasn't a normal brigand," he thought. They obviously moved all too well and quietly with cold, calculated precision.

He took notice that the other dark figure in the brush on the adjacent side of him wasn't moving at all but lay still.

"He is staying hidden as an invisible back up," thought Bren.

Involuntarily his eyes scrunched and his brow curled down at contemplating the fact and becoming surprised that there were humans that seemed to be working with the Margahns in attacking the camp. This was rarely heard of or seen in this day and age. Even the vilest of rogues and bandits of Attera only had small dealings with the despicable and unpredictable Margahns.

Movement caught his attention pulling him from his thoughts. He suddenly realized the black figure to his left was now expertly notching an arrow in his bow that was without any doubt being aimed towards Joshen's position!

A heavily impacting realization hit him at once that shook him to the core.

These two had seen Joshen move. Joshen had given away his position when he was contacting Bren with the secret hand language of the Ravenhawks. Again always quick at blaming himself first, Bren felt like if he hadn't been there, if Joshen hadn't been so protective of him, he wouldn't have had to move and be seen. He now painfully went from feeling like a useless burden to thinking he may be something quite worse, a liability that could cause his friends to make a deadly mistake that under normal circumstances they would have not. These "normal circumstances" he was referring to would be defined as the two veteran Ravenhawks doing their missions without worrying about the welfare of a novice scout.

The young Mejian also realized that these two dangerous figures hadn't noticed him because their obvious focus was moving into a position to where they could take out Joshen and aid the Margahn attack on the makeshift camp. Bren felt that this current new situation, that was now endangering Joshen and Lurandor, was completely his fault.

As the man in black drew his bow, he felt another stir in his heart.

"What can I do?! I can't fight in melee range with two grown men, especially two at this obviously high skill level!" Bren's mind began to race trying to think of a feasible plan.

"I'm just a kid who isn't old enough to be of any real use and shouldn't even be here. I can't even control my nerves, under normal circumstances, let alone be of any use in a tight pinch!" Bren was thinking again of when he failed his first Ravenhawk advancement test due to his "overactive nerves" as Joshen calls it. He felt like he lost control because of it and it continually weighed heavily on his confidence.

Bren was still just a Finch level scout, a beginning novice rank in the Ravenhawks. His olive green knit Ravenhawk hat with finch feathers sticking out the back, that now kept sweat from pouring in his eyes, reminded him of that fact daily.

He knew he had to do something. Deep down he knew Joshen hadn't discovered the presence of these skillful attackers who were an unforeseen threat to their whole plan.

"I was supposed to stay up here, out of harm's way and

do my part, and now I'm in the thick of it. This was not the plan. This is not how it is supposed to be," he thought with his usual ill-fated pessimism. "There is nothing fair in the world."

Inside he felt the hammer slam into his spirit and crush him on the anvil of sobering reality.

After all, he was just a child of twelve winters. Many young adults would have cracked already under the strain of such a situation.

"If these two attack me, I will die in seconds. I am just a small bug to be squished against a foe of this size and skill."

He didn't even think he could get to the sword on his back to attack quickly enough to do any good with a surprise strike against the perceived skill of these two.

"If I don't act, Joshen will be ambushed in a sneak attack."

He thought of grabbing an impact bomb and hitting the black figure, but he knew the blast would kill them both.

"Again another hopeless option," Bren concluded. "If I stood and threw the bombs at the approaching Margahns as planned, the black attacker would still probably kill Joshen with a surprise arrow and the two would then make quick work of me.

"The only good part of that plan was that maybe a few Margahns would die. But this was a no go plan too," thought Bren, becoming more frustrated with each passing second.

Time waits on no one, and his allotted time was running out, and running out quickly. He strained his mind. He knew he had only a few fleeting moments to weigh his options and pick the best thing to do. It was only a matter of seconds before the Margahns would reach the camp. Bren knew, at that point, the black figure would lose his arrow and attack Joshen while he prepared and focused his attention to shoot the Margahns as they drew near.

Joshen and Robnob had both trained Bren in the subtle skill of looking at all possibilities when trying to find a solution to a seemingly unanswerable problem.

"More times than not, you will find that no problem is unsolvable if you never give up and patiently take the time to think it all the way through," Robnob the Gnome had told Bren this not long ago.

"But time is what I need now and don't have much of it left," Bren answered in his mind the voice of Nob that had leapt from his memories.

He was now in a place where anything he could think of doing would end in his death and possibly Joshen's as well. Time was running out and he had seconds to decide.

The anvil was pounding harder as Bren's heart thumped in sync and with the same tenacity and force.

A cold sweat came over him. He felt helpless. He was truly in the worst possible position that he could be. Even if he could leave his mentors (who were really more his closest thing to a family outside Robnob and Reyva that he had) and attempt to run for it, he would die in seconds from the hands of these two. How could he even think such thoughts? Fear always affected a person's mind in strange ways. Sometimes the motivation of self-preservation overrides all rational thought. Frustration and hopelessness attacked his thoughts as he came to the full haunting realization that he truly was in one of the most dangerous predicaments anyone could be in with the least amount of options to choose from and none of them leaving good odds he would survive it.

Having ruled out the bombs and the sword on his back, running away and leaving his two mentors was unthinkable despite his fear. In his anxiety and rattled thoughts, he had forgotten about the ring blade that sat in a holster strap around his boot. A ring blade is a six-inch, double-bladed knife with a ring on the end for spinning and changing grips used by the Ilbri and the Ravenhawk scouts of the descendants of the legendary forefather of their people, Mejia Levan. Little by little, Bren slipped his arm down and slowly brought his knee up at the same time, meticulously bringing his hand and the ring blade in his boot together. He was careful not to make a sound because a faulty movement now would surely mean his death.

Bren's index finger slipped into the ring at the end of the ring blade. He noticed his hand was shaking. He was fighting from quaking in fear. He was feeling mortified but he had to do something. He worried that fear was slowly overtaking his body.

Using a Ring Blade

"I don't wanna die... Heroes don't feel fear... I'm a coward... I've failed so many times... My nerves have always ruined me at everything I've ever tried, at everything I've ever wanted to do," his thoughts ran a muck in his mind. He found himself once again remembering his recent failures with deep shame and frustration.

"Why do I feel so much anxiety? Why does it overtake me so swiftly?" Bren questioned himself out of sure frustration knowing he couldn't find an answer.

But this time he realized he wasn't going to lose a free fighting match or archery shoot off. If his nerves took control now and mastered him, then Joshen would die, as well as Lurandor and himself.

"Be still and trust," he heard again. A voice both familiar and strange sounding new and yet ancient had spoken to him.

Now Bren was deep and drowning in panic; his innards fluttering from fear;

his mind lost in a darkness born of hopelessness. For a second, when all control of his being was lost to him in a chaotic spell of paralyzing fear, he became still. For no reason within the logic of understanding, within the bounds of his twelve-year old mind, he became still. At that moment, the Margahns reached the edge of the camp and waited.

Their first movement of attack came with a large jingrol jumping high off the ground with its fourteen-foot body stretched out in midair. The jingrol then came down with a roar as it crushed its belly and massive weight along with it into the tent of the campsite. Its intentions were to flatten the tent and kill the sleeping inhabitants, smashing them underneath its great weight. The jingrol landed with a large thud and then screamed like the thunder. The Margahns cheered and stormed the camp with swords and spears drawn charging towards what they thought were soon to be their helpless victims who were sleeping covered in travelers' blankets around the fire. They also mistakenly thought the jingrol was wailing from the animal passion of murdering the victims of the tent. Margahns weren't known for their impressive cognitive abilities.

Being too consumed in the thrill of attack and blood lust, they hadn't noticed the wooden spears that were protruding through the jingrol's now bleeding back. Joshen and Lurandor had foreseen this attack and had come across enough camp sites where hunters had met that fate of a jingrol attack, never waking up from their sleep. They had placed the wooden spears in the ground and hid them inside the roof-cover of the makeshift tent. The yells from the jingrol weren't the victory shouts of murder from the huge monster; they were the yells of death as the jingrol squirmed in horrific pain. It had impaled itself and was now skewered and caught by more than a dozen wooden spears sticking from the earth. This part of the plan worked well. The stupid Margahns, unaware of the jingrol's fate, didn't notice the trap yet as they charged the camp from the cover of the mist and high grasses of the meadow.

Now Bren was sparked by some strength deep inside him that, at the moment, he didn't know from where it came. He moved as fast as he could into the blur of action. It wasn't a plan and he was no longer thinking of outcome or consequences. His body was just moving. Instinct and trained skills took over as he swung the ring blade out of his boot holster toward the black figure that now had his arrow drawn back and aimed at Joshen's position atop the stone pillar across the other side of the camp. Instead of striking the attacker, Bren swung the ring blade on the end of his finger in a circular, lateral arc that severed the bow string. The tensed bow violently snapped and the black figure grunted in surprise and shock as it threw him off balance. The snap of the bow string briefly stunned the black figure. This enabled Bren to land his second attack on the now off-balanced larger opponent. Bren had spun his body with the lateral direction swing of his ring blade attack. As his entire body had turned in the spinning momentum, he swung his foot around and with his full weight behind it, he landed a blow with his foot right into the buttock of the man in black. The swing of the aimed blade attack and the spinning heel kick done together in a single twirling motion was a move that few free fighters his age could brag of pulling off in practice, let alone in combat.

"It worked," thought Bren surprised.

Bren couldn't believe it actually did, as the man was falling off the small cliff towards the camp below. The weight of the opponent being double Bren's twelve-year old frame had caused a strong rebounding shockwave as a result of his spin kick. It knocked Bren backwards into the opposite direction, causing him to fall back flat out in the air parallel with the ground. And that was what saved him.

The masked attacker was able to recover in midair as he was kicked off the cliff. Before he started to fall from the cliff, in one motion, with speed faster than the flick of an eye, he was able to draw his sword, twist around, and swing it while completing a full spin. The counter move would have cut any attacker in half, except for Bren who was luckily flying flat back in the air. The blade of the attacker in black skimmed across his chest. He felt the wind from it as it went over his face.

If Bren hadn't been knocked back and flat in the air from the rebound of his kick, he would have been cut in two. More than blind fate seemed to be at work here. The attacker in black had planned on striking a standing assailant who had hit him with the kick. Bren's unexpected lateral fall was all that saved his life. He hit the ground among the brush atop the small cliff above camp as the black figure turned and prepared to land in the middle of the makeshift camp. He couldn't believe what he just saw, the mysterious man's counterattack. He was both stunned and terrified at the skill of the black masked attacker.

"How was he able within the flash of an eye to recover in midair, draw his sword, and spin attack before he started to fall into the open air below him?" Bren wondered.

Bren didn't have more than a second to be thankful and reflect on the recent blur of events or ponder the ramifications of fate or blind luck. Looking up into the sky from where he landed and hit the ground on his back, he saw that the other attacker in black was on top of him in the air, sword drawn and aiming straight down at him. Bren's short life flashed before him as he raised his hand to block. He knew he couldn't get his ring blade in front of him in time for any type of defensive move. On his back, out-sized, and no way to move out of the way in time since his body was just feeling the jar from the fall, Bren knew he was dead.

The instant before the black masked attacker's blade was an inch from his heart, the attacker's head exploded in blue sparks and lighting like white flames. Bren saw a familiar arrow shaft's feather end for a split second as the arrow blast spun the attacker in the air and knocked him back a few feet to land in the brush. The attacker in black went into the next world not knowing he had left this one.

Bren took a deep breath and looked to see that his would be attacker hit the ground near him rolling through the weeds with an arrow in his head, burning with light blue flames. Bren then turned his head to look across the camp and saw Lurandor with bow in hand sitting on the adjacent pillar stone from Joshen's perch. Through the fog, Bren could see Lurandor's golden locks as his hood sat pulled back on his shoulders. His face had a faint glow of which only the Ilbri had when they called upon their inner strength when they fought evil. As the radiance of his face penetrated the fog, he looked up and nodded to Bren. Bren nodded back showing he was okay.

Lurandor had a green woven chord headband that held his golden hair back from his face exposing another unique feature of his people: their pointed elf-like ears. Out of the back of his green head band hung two beautiful griffin feathers; a symbol of the Ilbri from the world of Hollinedan, his people. Lurandor drew another arrow in a blur of quick motion, and looked down at the camp below. Meanwhile Bren sprung to his feet and watched as the Margahns attacked, hacking and slashing what they thought were sleeping hunters. The dying screams from the jingrol had filled the air with a loud wailing and grunting noise that covered and masked many surrounding sounds that kept them from noticing or hearing the motions of Lurandor and Bren. The ones that saw the black masked attacker landing from off the cliff thought he was coming down from his position to join in their massacre of the camp. Screaming battle cries from the shear excitement and anticipation of murdering helpless victims, the Margahns still didn't know they were in the clutches of a trap. They were truly stupid creatures, blinded by their blood lust and the promise of treasures and loot the raid would bring.

Not taking the time to even catch a breath, Bren reached in his pouch and unleashed a flurry of impact bombs. They exploded as they landed hitting the ground in the area of the camp. A score of unaware Margahns were blown to pieces or knocked down by the shock-waves from the thunderous impacts. The screams of blood-lust turned into the screams of fear as impact bombs exploded among their ranks all around the camp.

Lurandor was already at work. Arrows streaked through the fog taking down any Margahn who hadn't made it into the camp. His Ilbri eyes, unlike human eyes, could see through almost any natural fog or darkness. The Margahns, who could see in pitch black, couldn't see far in this fog, but not so for one of the children of the Ilbri whose eyes rivaled that of any hawk. Many Margahns who hadn't reached the camp turned and ran across the foggy meadow, after hearing and seeing the explosions, hoping the mist would cover their flight as they frantically tried to reach the protection of the line of trees of the nearby forest. The explosions had scared them so much that many were yelling in their own hideous tongue, screaming that the God of the light and fire, the protector of the good folk of Attera had fallen upon them. The stupid mongrel Margahns had never seen impact bombs at work before.

Fleeing did little good as they ran through the fog trampling through the high grass. They had no idea that the fog didn't hide them from the eyes of Lurandor, an Ilbri. A few spread out and hid behind the stone monoliths; some might have actually escaped had they been smart enough to fly in different directions. Instead they all ran in one direction, yelling and howling being the wild goblin-ape-hyenas that they were, knocking over each other as they were only in fear for their own selfish lives. Within seconds, almost all were lying dead burning from the blue-fire flames of Lurandor's arrows. One of the fleeing Margahns had almost reached the edge of the forest across the far side of the meadow. From where Lurandor sat atop his monolith stone pillar, the far side of the meadow would have been blurry at best to the seeing distance of a human, but not the eyes of an Ilbri. In his hand was a bow made of the mighty Luthuwan tree, a tree not native to Attera. The Ilbri had brought the Luthuwan seeds with them when they came to Attera ages ago, fleeing from their dying home world Hollinedan. The wood from these trees made bows that had no rival compared to any other type of wood found in Attera. Lurandor pulled his Luthuwan bow, paused a second, making some quick calculations in his head, and then fired an arrow. It arched across the meadow, rising above the fog. At its apex, for an instant in time, the arrow caught and reflected the gleam of a red glow from the rays of the early morning sun. After it peaked and reached the height of its flight, it then dropped back into the fog and found its running, screaming target. The shot was something worthy of a bard's legendary tale and was exceptionally amazing to execute, even for an Ilbri. Lurandor, in his skilled estimation, had measured a great distance times the speed of the Margahn and launched his arrow that dropped the running Margahn with a head shot. There wasn't another archer in Attera that could even make boast of a claim at such a shot. Standing firm and tall, the Ilbri dropped his cloak from around him letting it float off his stone perch to the ground. Lurandor's earthen green tunic shimmered in the morning sun as its rays broke through the dense fog to pour sunshine radiance upon the flowered meadows. It appeared that the foggy mist seemed to dissipate as Lurandor revealed the essence of his inner strength. The ancient power of the spirit of his timeless people visibly glowed from him in an aura around his body. Bren, who had already thrown his last bomb, stood atop the cliff. He had done his part, and breathing heavily from his adrenaline-spent body, he watched Lurandor, the Ilbri warrior, in his power now fully revealed standing on top of the stone. A few surviving Margahns around the now burning camp looked up squinting at the morning light and saw their impending doom. Some yelled, screaming in Margukh, the Margahn language, for the Dead Jin to help them, hoping that would change their fate.

Chapter 3

A SHADE IN THE WOODS

Joshen watched the black masked figure fall off the small cliff after Bren blindsided him with a spin kick. Joshen then burst forth from his crouched position on top of the stone monolith and landed softly on the ground below. The black figure fell skillfully to his feet among the ruckus of the fake makeshift camp. He then zigzagged around the disoriented Margahns, and swiftly made his way out of the clearing of the meadow to the edge of the tree line.

The Ravenhawk chief pushed himself forward, going as fast as his legs and feet could manage. Just as he was approaching the edge of the meadow, a Margahn that was crouched low hiding, sprang from the tall thick grass, square in front of Joshen as he was running full speed. The creature hoped it had caught its victim unaware and off guard. It thought Joshen was fleeing scared and helpless from the attack. It, as you well know, thought wrong on both matters. A mistake it would not live to repeat to have the opportunity to correct. The Margahn had a spear in its hands and right away thrust it straight at Joshen's midsection. The Margahn was thinking that Joshen could not stop his momentum going forward or be able to draw a weapon out in time to do a counter defensive move. Joshen, without losing a stride in mid run, simply brought up his split toe tabi boot and kicked under the thrusting spear, hitting the staff so hard that it was ripped right out of the Margahn's hands and went flying nearly twenty feet over its head landing behind it somewhere in the trees of the nearby forest. Before the ugly, canine-looking creature could even realize what just occurred and ponder where and what happened to its crude spear, Joshen drew his curved Mejian sword and cut the mongrel down with a fast swipe, slashing it across its midsection. Another Margahn had gotten behind him as soon as he had stopped to take down the one with the spear in front of him with his sword slash. It growled and barked with glee like a hyena, as it leaped towards him to attack his back. In its left hand, it had a metal c-shaped hook called a "devil claw." It swung the devil claw out planning to drive it deep into Joshen's back, the way a market butcher would hook meat up, and hang it in the window of his shop. In its right hand, it had a crudely made blade that looked like it was just a slab of sharpened black metal with a wrapped handle. The Margahn planned to hook him with the devil claw and hold him still while it cut and carved him up, butchering Joshen from behind as he would not be able to turn with the hook in his back. Joshen had many years battle experience; he trained and conditioned himself to always keep an eye on his backside flank. This was why he caught a glimpse of the Margahn over his left shoulder as his sword completed its arc as he had swung it in the same direction. Joshen's body followed the path of the sword strike and side stepped in a circular pattern. The devil claw hook swung down and hit nothing but air as Joshen now had strategically positioned himself behind the left back side of the Margahn with his savvy spinning combat footwork. He did this wisely; had he spun in the other direction, he might have turned right into the range of the Margahn's crude sword that was in its right hand. As the Margahn's hand had swung down with its devil claw hook almost reaching the ground, unable to stop the momentum from its complete miss, Joshen brought his sword over and chopped its hand off which went flying.

The devil claw hook's point stuck in the ground with the Margahn's hairy severed hand still gripping it. Before it could even get a whimper out, Joshen changed the momentum and direction of his blade and severed its ugly, beastly looking head, clean from its shoulders. Prior to its head hitting the ground, Joshen was off running again, knowing he was pressed for time and didn't have a moment to spare.

It was apparent the shadowed figure was done with his part helping the Margahns in the battle. Ignoring the wailing cries of his dying mongrel allies, he made his way to the forest, hoping it would provide cover for his escape. As he disappeared into the shelter of the trees, an earthen-cloaked man followed him, closing the distance between them with great dexterity and speed.

As Joshen entered into the forest, he saw the black figure just ten paces ahead of him running at a good, fast pace. Joshen knew he had to catch the mysterious man quickly before he lost him in the thick woods, or before he lost his breath chasing him. The old Ravenhawk wasn't able to run great distances as he did in his youth. Still, Joshen pushed his well-aged body hard, trying to muster as much speed as he could maintain. It was well-known that a skilled Ravenhawk scout can pursue a deer running at a near full speed trot and grasp it by its tail, before the deer heard his footsteps or even knew it was being chased. Joshen was an expert in his craft; a chief-level Ravenhawk scout whose mastery of the group's scouting skills was legendary throughout Attera. As he ran onward driving his body forward, he steadied his breath and expertly chose his footing with each stride, making no more noise running across the forest floor than a mild breeze might make disturbing the leaves. Joshen gained ground on his fast moving target. Stealthily he kept running behind the fleeing masked being in black, all the while using all his senses trying to determine if he had been noticed by his masked prey.

Without losing a single stride or breaking rhythm in his fast-paced run and not giving any hint that might reveal his attack, the masked man in black twisted in mid run and flung three metal throwing spikes straight backwards, flying true and straight to their mark, Joshen's head.

Running at near full speed, the seasoned Ravenhawk scout was almost caught off guard. This unexpected attack forced him to react instantly. It would have been very unlikely, even for someone as skilled as Joshen, to successfully block all three spikes at once. Running forward at full speed made it impossible for Joshen to side step or twist out of the way to avoid the spikes that were expertly flying directly towards him. There was also no time to draw the sword from his back to use as a deflective shield, and he knew better than to stop the spikes with his bare arms as a last resort defensive move. Experience has taught him that small weapons of this sort are often tainted with poison. So the veteran Ravenhawk chief did the most natural counter possible that he could pull off at a full run. He fell straight back, causing his body to drop down horizontally to the forest floor. The three spikes flew over him, narrowly missing his body, but finding homes in nearby trees.

The spikes sizzled and hissed when they drove deep into the bark of the trees they hit. This demonstrated beyond doubt that they were in fact poisoned as the Ravenhawk chief had believed them to be.

In avoiding the spikes, Joshen had stuck his feet straight out and with the momentum from his run, slid nearly four feet forward after the spikes flew past his head. The leafy forest floor created quite an efficient sliding surface. As his slide neared the end, Joshen used the last of the momentum to sit up from the slide and leapt forward with all his might, diving toward the running man in black. Joshen's sliding leap was just enough to reach his intended goal. As he flew through the air, stretching with all his might and his arm fully extended, he caught the black figure's ankle, causing him to trip.

However, instead of falling, the black figure rolled, breaking the impact against the ground. In an amazing display of agility, as he rolled, he effortlessly unsheathed his short, straight-bladed katana, midway through his acrobatic maneuver. As he finished his roll, he planted his feet and reversed his momentum, jumping back toward Joshen who still lay flat out from the dive. The assassin grinned from under his mask, as he came down swinging his straight katana with both hands, putting all of his weight into the strike, determined to split Joshen in two.

He knew Joshen couldn't draw his sword in time to block or roll out of the way. The Mejian scout had landed on his back from twisting when he grabbed the assassin's leg. His sword was pinned in the sheath between his back and the ground, and he could not draw it in time while in this prone position. Joshen raised his left arm to cross his chest and supported it from underneath with his right. The assassin ignored this last attempt at a defense from his downed Mejian opponent. He would sever both arms and slash his sword through Joshen's chest, driving it through all the way to the ground. The assassin in black raised his sword over his head and with blinding speed, swung it in a lightning fast arc aiming at the prostrate Ravenhawk.

"Cling!" was the sound that echoed from metal to metal violently meeting. It rang in the masked figure's ears, surprising him, and the impact shook him up since he was planning on hitting and slicing through flesh and bone. During his dive, Joshen had unsheathed his ring blade with the hand opposite the one with which he grabbed the black figure's ankle. He had stuck his finger through the metal circle at the end of his ring blade and pulled it from his boot. With his index finger through the metal ring at the pommel of the dagger, the blade now lay flat against his arm, hidden under his tunic sleeve. Placing the flat side of the blade like this, tightly against his forearm, gave Joshen a thick layer of metal armor over his unprotected limb. The maneuver was called the "Hidden Guard Technique." This was a blocking method the Ravenhawk scouts practiced that utilized the ring blade as a metal shield to block sword attacks.

The black figure was jarred by the unsuspecting block; the jarring, unforgiving impact, of metal on metal caused a hard jolt to shake through his body. Putting all of his force into a single strike was a mistake, and in an instant, Joshen took full advantage. He grinned as he imagined the shocked expression hidden behind the mask of the darkly dressed figure's face. From his back, Joshen kicked up with his right foot, smashing the man square in the face. Knocked back a good six feet, the assassin went rolling backwards over his shoulder, tucking his neck, and came up to sit on one knee. Joshen skillfully then kipped up, landing on his feet, and with his right hand, he drew his curved, single-edged, dragon head-chopper sword (a short, broad, curved-bladed sword that is widely used by and taught to the Mejian members of the Ravenhawk scouts). With his sword drawn, he then turned to face his masked opponent who was crouched on one knee with his sword held in a defensive position.

Swelling could be seen on both sides of the assassin's nose through the eye slits of his mask. Joshen noticed both he and his masked opponent were both

breathing heavily. In silence, each scrutinized the other, spying for weaknesses and strengths. While analyzing the situation, Joshen felt the intensity of the "fight or flight" adrenaline rush lessen in his body. He knew he had to end this battle soon, or the advantage would greatly begin to sway giving much favor to his younger, very dangerously skilled opponent.

As was expected, he didn't need to wait long. In the middle of a breath, the black clad figure hissed like a snake. Until this point, Joshen hadn't realized that his opponent was some sort of conjurer or spell user. The black clad figure hissed a strange serpent-like sound that resonated into the words of an ancient incantation. He lifted his right hand and tattooed on the palm were old Sarnian cult symbols and runes that began to glow with a pulsing bright green light. Joshen prepared himself quickly, as he knew that a magical attack was being contrived to be used against him.

A green flame appeared over the masked man's hand. Drawing power from the phantom spirits that dwelt in and infested his body, he used their spiritual energies and power to successfully conjure what was called a "poison-fire sphere."

The poisonous orb of flame hovered above his hand as he reached back stretching his arm out and threw it in a quick flash of a movement. Crackling and screeching, it flew through the air in a straight line destined to collide with Joshen's head, moving as would a bright comet soaring across a darkened night sky. Just barely in time, Joshen used the flat part of his broad blade and knocked the green burning sphere to the side, sending it flying through the woods, scorching bark and leaf along with everything else in its path. Green hued, poison-fire sphere conjuring is a common battle spell used among Shamans. Its unholy cured flames would have poisoned as well as severely burned Joshen if he had even slightly come in contact with it. The black figure moved in quickly, following directly behind the flame he sent and was instantly in melee combat range with Joshen. Right away the two were locked in combat that began with a blinding barrage of attacks, counters and re-counters. The would-be assassin maneuvered his blade effortlessly, skillfully attacking Joshen's center and both his flank sides with such speed that it seemed the bladed strikes fell almost simultaneously. Moving with deadly cunning and precision, the masked foe in black kept changing attack patterns, varying in direction, angles, and heights, put Joshen on his heels before he could muster any type of counter-offensive. Few warriors in all of Attera have ever driven Joshen back, forcing him into a battle mode of purely self-protective defensive fighting motions. The dark figure, noticing he had the Ravenhawk scout busy parrying his multiple sword strikes, pressed the intensity of his attack with more speed and strength. While he had the advantage, the dark figure looked for a weakness in Joshen's tight defensive postures and forms.

Joshen used his ring blade hidden guard block to defend against strikes that targeted his left flank. With his other side, he used a single-arm sword style to fend off his assailant's varied, lightning-fast attacks on his right flank.

After surviving the assailant's deadly offensive, Joshen, using superb defensive martial techniques, was able to rebound from the attacks and recover enough to start his own counter-offensive movements. He alternately blocked and attacked with the ring blade and swung with his dragon head-chopper sword at the masked man, driving the black figure back with an overwhelming storm of spinning and jabbing strikes. Joshen previously had plans of capturing the black clad figure for questioning, but knew now that he was too dangerous. With an honestly sobering analysis of the situation, the battle seasoned Mejian realized that he would be hard-pressed just to kill his opponent, if he could even accomplish that.

The black figure, while being driven back, saw an opening in the Ravenhawk Chief's nearly flawless defenses. Joshen's fast pressing attack had left his sword arm high, exposing his chest. The black figure took the opportunity and thrust the katana straight at Joshen's exposed right flank. At the very last moment, just as the blade would have pierced his chest, the black figure realized, unable to stop his movement at this point, that he had fallen for a well-devised trap. It was a risky, difficult move to attempt, but Joshen knew the longer the battle went on the more it worked against his favor. The Mejian scout had easily concluded he would run out of strength and fuel to keep fighting much more quickly than his obviously younger opponent, who didn't need any physical energy at all to keep casting wicked combat spells against Joshen long after his endurance failed.

With a combination of footwork and hip motion, Joshen twisted his body so that the black assailant's sword went by him harmlessly. This combination move got him safely out of the way, off the center line path of the katana sword that was jabbing straight along, aiming to pierce and thrust through his midsection. Joshen strategically, in the same maneuver, moved his right hand holding the sword, displaying an amazing demonstration of skill. He precisely placed the ring on the pommel of his sword in perfect alignment with the oncoming sword thrust towards him from his opponent. This caused the katana blade to go straight through the large ring at the end of the dragon head-chopper's handle. Joshen then twisted around and used his forearm, which was protected by the ring blade, to knock the katana from his opponent's hands, slamming the flat part of the blade into the black figure's wrist at a specific place that perfectly assaulted the nerves of the hand. Joshen had expertly performed a nerve point attack.

Joshen then grabbed the handle of the katana and spun in the same direction he had twisted before in his defensive move. With his ring blade hand gripping the dark figure's weapon just below the guard, Joshen was now also controlling the direction of the tip of the katana's blade while it was still trapped in his sword handle's ring. He twisted, spinning completely around, and drove the dark-masked figure's own sword deep into his chest. The man was dead before he hit the ground. As his body thudded against the ground, several black specters that were nearly transparent left the dead man's body. With glowing red eyes, one paused in front of Joshen's face and looked at him for a second, then with a low sounding hiss, it flew off into the shadows of the forest as a snake would swim through water.

Joshen, in disgust, mumbled out loud, "Cursed Sarn spirit! Go back to hide in the dark bowls of Attera!"

Joshen then fell to one knee, exhausted and still breathing heavily. He rested as best he could as he inhaled large amounts of air with each breath. Once he caught his breath, he solemnly recited an ancient prayer to Ya-El, the All Creator that had been historically spoken by the Mejian tribes since before their forefather Leban walked the lands of Mejia with his sons.

The path I took this day
Has taken a life away
I pray this path was right, the only one I could have taken
May it be a work of light, and that I am not mistaken
May the road have no bends, and still lead me to the eternal blessed fountain
Shepherding me to walk the winds, guiding me to your Celestial Sacred Mountain
I pray lead my feet, light all my ways to where your throne does lie
With speed to meet, right when all my days are gone and have said goodbye

With a deep voice, in the tune of an ancient melody he cantered this prayer that had been passed down orally for generations among the tribes of his people. Joshen sang this prayer with his head bowed in the ancient Mejian tongue.

After his prayer and a brief pause, he then quickly examined the black figure's remains looking for any clues or information that may prove to be useful later.

"Only a brief moment should be used here…I need to make haste or I fear I may be too late to help Lurandor and Bren back at the meadow," thought Joshen as he was deeply worried about how his two companions were faring.

He quickly searched the body of his dead foe and found an assortment of weapons and devices. His eyes widened slightly as he realized what he was looking at. He found on the strange black clad man rarely seen equipment.

"These gear and weapons are native for the most part, only to Jin Go Mei,"* Joshen said to himself in partial disbelief. This discovery led to a bunch of questions that started to gather in his head, even though he had already guessed that the black clad assailant was a trained Shade Warrior,* a warrior class from the Orient. His guess was now no longer just educated speculation, but now it was confirmed.

"No time to figure this mystery out and appropriately find where all the pieces of this puzzle properly fit… no time now at all… I must get back to Lurandor and Bren."

Then Joshen was met with a second surprise, as his hand reached inside a secret inner pocket of the fallen man's oriental crossed-style tunic. His hand suddenly felt warm and tingly.

"Hmm…," thought Joshen. "What is this?"

It felt like a polished stone on the surface, but heat and energy seemed to emanate from it. It almost appeared to hum or vibrate gently as if it had a life of its own.

Joshen gasped as he pulled out the mysterious object. It was a transparent looking stone, but had multiple hues of light that swirled translucently in the

Tinkmut's Gazetteer and Encyclopedia of Attera

THE KINGDOMS, TOWNS, AND VILLAGES OF ATTERA

Excerpt, added and written by Robnob Haborav - Woodland Gnome and Scholar Sage

THE LANDS OF JIN GO MEI – Jin Go Mei is the name for the oriental continent and islands that are located across the East Oriental Ocean from Attera. The three largest kingdoms of the Eastern Orient are:

Mei – the largest kingdom of the Orient, located in the center continent, is made of two provinces, Chong, and to its North, Mong.

Jin – the second largest in size, located in the North West.

Go – the third largest kingdom, located on a group of islands just off the Western coast of Mei in the East Oriental Ocean.

Tinkmut's Gazetteer and Encyclopedia of Attera

WORKING CLASSES OF ATTERA

Excerpt, added and written by Robnob Haborav - Woodland Gnome and Scholar Sage

SHADE WARRIOR (NINJA CLASS) – The Ninja pofessional warrior class origins are shrouded in secrecy and myth. Most Ninja are trained and work through highly covert guilds that are more akin to family clans or sworn brotherhoods. They are highly skilled in combat, stealth, specialized weaponry, unorthodox warfare, spying and espionage, hired or warfare assassins, and much more.

In the Land of Go, there are two main factions that have been at war with each other for many ages: the Kage No Senshi, from the province of Koga, and the Shinobi, from the province of Iga. The Kage No Senshi are often in Attera and Jin Go Mei. They are simply called "shades." They are maliciously evil and merciless. They have well-known wicked reputations and are greatly feared by the good folk of Jin Go Mei. Shades frequently use and are often willfully possessed by Shedim (demon) spirits that aid them in spell casting, warfare, espionage and assassinations for which they are known. The shade warriors are usually highly skilled warriors as well as warlocks, shamans, or necromancers.

cont...

...cont

The Shinobi – This group of Ninja from the land of Iga use their skills for the good of the people and their kingdoms. They serve as professional spies, body guards and special elite fighting forces supporting local townships, provinces and area lords. They often are devout sages gaining strength and aid from the Creator Ya-El who they call "Shang-di." They detest and shun the evil magical, spiritual practices of their rival ninja faction the Kage No Senshi.

Tinkmut's drawing of a Shade Warrior assassin.

center.

"If light took the form of water," Joshen whispered to himself, "this is what it would look like."

"What in the Eight Kingdoms is this strange stone that emanates life-like energy?" Joshen wondered as he carefully tucked it in his side pouch.

He also saw a strange tattoo on the man's inner wrist. It was of a symbol he could not read or decipher but knew it was from one of the ancient languages spoken from the oriental lands of Jin Go Mei. No time to look for more things or answers now; he knew he had to get back to the smoldering campsite. He'd already been gone too long. He was praying that no evil had befallen Bren or Lurandor during his absence. He also prayed that he had chosen the right path in following the masked warrior into the forest. With that in mind, he rose up and started to run, pushing his tired legs to work much harder than they wanted to go.

As Joshen reached the edge of the forest, a familiar messenger bird intercepted him along the path.

Chapter 4

A MEADOW, A MARGAHN, AND AN ILBRI

Lurandor laid his bow down and nimbly leaped from his stone pillar. He quickly scanned the campsite and saw that most of the Marghans lay dead around him from the initial onslaught of arrows and explosions. Lurandor grabbed the spear he had hidden among the green leaf vines growing up the sides of the stone monolith.

As the spear settled in the palm of his hands, two surviving Marghans were on him. Armed with a crude cleaver sword and a spiked club, the Marghans positioned on his front and back sides tried attacking at once. They hoped to catch him at a disadvantage, surrounded as he was, naively thinking he could not defend both attacks at once. Again Marghans were never known for having exceptional cognitive abilities. This mistake would be the last they ever made. Had they been intelligent enough to assess Lurandor's skills, they would have wisely turned and run. Lurandor exploded into motion. With the butt of his spear, he scooped dirt and earth and flung it into the face of his front-side attacker. As the spear leveled from the flinging movement, he slid his left hand to his right, thrusting the spear backwards as his body twisted, catching the surprised Marghan behind him in the face. The spiked club that the Marghan held up for a strike fell as his arm limply dropped. Before the Marghan to his front side even recovered from the earth clumps in his face, Lurandor turned and swung his spear in a full arc, slashing the Marghan with the sharp outside edge of his foot-long spearhead blade.

He then brought the spear to his side in a defensive posture. In the same instant, both Marghans collapsed; their eyes seeing the darkness of death before they hit the ground. Lurandor scanned again all around the fake campsite. There was no movement. Smoke and mist filled the open meadow; remnants of the impact bombs' deadly effectiveness. Lurandor relaxed his readiness seeing that no living combatants were left.

Suddenly he sensed something amiss, "Chanting." Lurandor's keen ears heard the unmistakable utterances of an incantation.

"A Margahn shaman for sure," Lurandor thought out loud. "He must be hiding in the tall grass blanketed by smoke and mist."

In most cases, Lurandor's eyes could see through fog and darkness but not through all the smoke created by the burning weeds and brush that caught fire from Bren's impact bomb explosions.

His spiritual discernment fired off and in an instant, Lurandor dove behind one of the stone monoliths, putting it between him and the chanting, and did so barely in time. The whole area he had been standing in exploded in green and black flames. Lurandor felt the heat from the flames as they partially wrapped around the stone he used as a makeshift shield. If he had hesitated for only a brief moment, he would have been burned instantly into ash and cinder.

"I can't see him through the smoke and mist. If one of those spell blasts finds me, I'll suddenly find myself as a spirit walking the winds heading towards the path around the Sacred Mountain leading to Ya-El's throne."

With an extreme feat of agility, Lurandor climbed the vines with one arm holding his spear. He swiftly reached the top of the monolith he was previously on and grabbed his bow.

"Only two arrows left. Not good."

The chanting started again.

"I still can't see him. Where are you hiding Shaman?" He whispered to himself.

Lurandor had a grim smile on his face for a brief moment, "I know how to find you."

Lurandor strung an arrow, pulled it back and spoke in Ilbri, "Ya-El, light my arrow with your sacred flame."

The arrow head made from silver and teckal, a rare blue stone mix, sparked into blue and white flames. Lurandor shot the arrow in the direction of the chanting. The arrow lit as it flew over, exposing two different black outlines in the mist. Lurandor quickly shot his second and last arrow before the light of the first one went out. It exploded in flames as one of the outlined figures went down.

"Still chanting. Wrong one I guess. I missed the Shaman and that was my last arrow."

Lurandor leaped down as a black and red fireball blew off the top of the stone pillar.

"He is powerful in the dark arts... must be filled with many Shedim spirits. No time to waste," Lurandor thought as he hit the ground running. In a lightning fast move, he had cleared the distance to where the figure of the Shaman was last seen. His black form began to take shape through the smoke as Lurandor approached.

The Shaman's face snarled.

"Granack," he spoke in the vulgar Marghan language, and a black web shot from his hand, burning green with poison fire. Lurandor jumped and dove, barely missing the deadly web.

The shaman looked through the mist and high grass. "Where did the Ilbri go?" He thought.

The Margahn shaman began to panic. He knew the Ilbri was hiding somewhere in the waist deep grass. The Margahn conjurer chanted another spell and a green fire ball appeared in his hand. He was moving, turning and twisting in all directions. He knew that at close range he would die in hand to hand combat against an Ilbri. He turned to the left and then to the right not knowing where Lurandor was. Suddenly he felt his chest burning. Unable to scream, he looked down to see the spear of Lurandor sticking out of his chest, pierced from behind. His arms fell down and the green poison fire ball that he held in his hand, ready to be thrown, flickered out harmlessly. Maneuvering unseen in the high grass, Lurandor had circled behind him. He now kicked the dark fur-covered beast in the back and pulled out the foot-long head of his spear from the dead Margahn's back. Several black, faintly visible, semi-transparent Shedim (Sarn and Nephal) spirit forms left the Margahn shaman's corpse lying in the tall grass of the meadow, hissing as they scattered and fled to disappear into the shadows of the distant tree line.

As the smoke and mist cleared, Lurandor scouted out the area making sure the raiding party was completely eliminated.

"Bren! Area is clear. Come down now and let us find what is keeping our friend so occupied. I hope all is well," Lurandor spoke in his normal cheerful tones. He made sure his deep concern for Joshen wasn't evident in his speaking. He didn't want Bren to see that he was worried about Joshen which would more than likely cause their young apprentice to panic or at least become overly worried himself.

Moving at a steady pace, Bren made his way around the edge of the small cliff on which he had been positioned. The ridge eventually sloped off and he easily walked down and approached the camp area where Lurandor was standing. As he walked, the adolescent Mejian was pulling his hair back and putting his Ravenhawk scout knit hat back on that had fallen off during his skirmish with the black figures. Bren nervously fumbled with picking up the finch scout feathers that had fallen off to the ground and reattached them to his knit hat.

"After this morning's performance, I feel you will not be wearing that color of hat much longer and you will not need those finch feathers," laughed Lurandor, whose outlook never seemed to be upset or glum, despite just narrowly surviving a recent gruesome battle.

"Maybe," Bren replied, keeping his words few for fear Lurandor would hear the trembling in his voice. He still felt like he was shaking quite a bit. His nerves seemed to be radiating throughout his whole being, originating from his fluttering guts. Bren avoided eye contact while he continued to fumble with his green Ravenhawk hat still attempting to get his hair properly tucked in it. He sat down on a small log near the campfire as he felt weak and sick.

"I never thought a real battle would be this way," Bren thought. He learned that killing was a necessary action, if it saved more lives in the end. Bren learned this lesson hard that day. Today was the first time he saw a person killed, and he knew he would never be the same again. An important life event had happened at this moment and he failed to realize it at the time that another part of his naive childhood was now over. Whether he was ready or not, a new chapter had begun.

"Magnificent," Lurandor spoke as he was sheathing his spear head.

"Bren, your actions saved the day. Had you not reacted to the situation as you did, I feel this day would have turned out to be a bad one for us all," Lurandor, filled with pride for the apprentice he was helping Joshen train, praised Bren.

"Joshen and I always knew you had it in you. You took an impossible situation and made a way through it. That is the true mark of a Ravenhawk. The ability to remain resilient, resolved, and unwavering until what is deemed impossible is forced into the realm of possibilities by shear faith and determination. The dark men in black were not part of our plans and yet you were able to make a change in plans under such tight, precarious circumstances. I feel many veteran Ravenhawks would not have fared as well as you did against such a skilled, unknown foe."

Lurandor's praise did little to calm down Bren. The young Mejian sat down on a log and now stopped pretending to finagle with his hat only to start adjusting and readjusting the sheathed ring blade strapped to his boot, even though it needed no adjusting in any slightest way. He was afraid to look Lurandor in the eye. He wanted to hide from the Ilbri the fear that still gripped him. He kept his gaze downward as he mindlessly fiddled with his ring blade.

"He will see the fear in my eyes and read the story of my heart written in bold letters on my face," Bren thought to himself. He felt transparent as if Lurandor could see straight through him and look upon his innermost turmoil. Bren wished he was under the covers in his own bed. He missed his home. He missed the warm fires of Nob's tree home where he had grown up most of his life. He realized now how much he never fully appreciated the value of the security and peace that existed in the old gnomish tree house that he called home; the only home he ever knew.

Lurandor had already looked at Bren more than a few times, and with a quick glance, he intuitively sensed instantly that Bren was still really in a spiritual turmoil.

"Bren, cutting the bow string with your ring blade and following with a spin kick was magnificent! Continue moving like that and you will pass your next free-form fighting match easily along with completing the rest of the trials. You will be a full Ravenhawk apprentice for sure by the end of summer!" Lurandor said encouragingly.

Chapter 5

TALKING BIRDS AND FLYING SNAKES

Tinkmut's Gazetteer and Encyclopedia of Attera

VARIOUS FOLK, BEINGS, & CREATURES OF HOLLINEDAN

Excerpt, added and written by Tinkmut Badaboogs

RAVENHAWK BIRD FOLK—The Ravenhawk is also called "Black Hawk." This bird folk are a tall, midnight black-colored race of speaking, free-willed beings that resemble the large predator hawks native to Attera except they are quite large in comparison, standing between three and four feet in height. They usually speak several languages and dialects and are often employed by the Ravenhawk scouts as messengers flying continually back and forth between traveling squads on missions in the wild lands and Ravenlodge, the main home headquarters of the Mejian scouts. The Mejians had named their scouts after the Ravenhawk birds who had helped them tremendously be more efficient in operating their organization, supplying them with the fastest form of distant communication in Attera. The Ravenhawk were among the beings that followed the Ilbri through the Celestial Radiance portal, escaping the dying world of Hollinedan, coming to Attera as inter-world refugees.

A sketch of Kharvack drawn by Tinkmut Badaboogs

"Bren, let's not tarry here any longer. We must hurry! Joshen may need our help," Lurandor urged Bren as he shook his spear, readying it in his hand. "Caw! Caw!"

Lurandor and Bren both turned to see Joshen walking across the meadow clearing with a large three-foot, solid black Mejian Ravenhawk bird* perched on a thick leather wrap on Joshen's arm.

"Old friend, I fear we are all going to need help soon enough," declared Joshen with a grim smile.

Lurandor, who was startled at first by the sudden loud cawing, now breathed deeply and laughed, happy to see the weathered Ravenhawk chief's face in the late morning sun. Lurandor didn't stay happy too long as he saw the grim look of concern etched in Joshen's brow.

"Greetings Kharvack," spoke the Ilbri. "I see you have found us."

Kharvack cawed and cooed in answer.

"Yes, we had a fierce battle this day," replied Lurandor.

Joshen spoke something in Mejian to Kharvack. The large Ravenhawk bird cawed again and flew to the top of the nearby stone monolith and sat there, seeming to be looking and keeping his eye out for something in the distance.

Joshen walked toward Lurandor and Bren and sat down opposite from them, across the other side of the flickering embers of what was left of the burning campfire.

"So, were you able to catch the fleeing black figure or did the years of wear and tear catch up to you first?" Lurandor quipped.

"Though I'm not ageless like you, my old friend, I still have a lot of trail time left in this aging body," Joshen smiled as he wiped the sweat from his brow. "I caught him but was unable to keep from killing him."

Joshen told them of the black figure's skills and described their skirmish in detail.

"I was hard-pressed to beat him," Joshen said.

A look of shock slightly fell on Lurandor's face, as he replied, "Joshen, I don't know of any three warriors at once, from the Allowin River to the East Orient Ocean, who can match you at close range in combat."

"These masked figures' skills, as we both have more than likely concluded, come from Jin Go Mei, if I'm not wrong in guessing so."

Lurandor nodded in agreement.

"Not too many people in Attera know about, and even fewer have trained in, the ancient martial skills of Jin Go Mei. Yes, I fear these men, who are not from Jin Go Mei but have the look of men from the Eight Kingdoms of Attera, were trained by someone skilled in the shade warrior arts from the Far East Orient Islands. They were either trained in Jin Go Mei or by a rogue shade warrior from that land somewhere here in Attera."

"They are without a doubt the Jin Go Mei shade warriors, 'Kage No Senshi.'"

"Why are they here and who are they working with?" asked Joshen as much to himself as to everyone else.

"Their skill was great. They were more than just hired mercenaries. The one you killed, Bren had earlier caught off guard and kicked him off the cliff. The shade warrior was able to counterstrike in midair with deadly speed and accuracy. Few warriors in Attera are at that level, even among the Ilbri and Mejians."

"The one I shot with an arrow," Lurandor paused to reflect, "if I would have shot the arrow from a lesser bow whose wood was not made from a great Luthuwan tree, I fear he would have snatched my arrow out of the air! I was amazed when I saw it. He was in midair bent on attacking Bren, and still, his hand moved as fast as a Suthnian snake striking, almost catching my arrow. Had Bren not reacted how he did and Ya-El's light had not shined in our favor, the day's outcome may have turned out evil for us all."

Bren shuffled uneasily. He didn't feel like he deserved or was ready to handle any more compliments.

"Had he known the skill of his adversaries, would he have been able to overcome his almost paralyzing fears and done what he did?" Bren thought to himself.

"Two shade warriors in the mainland of Attera. I have never come across one before in all my travels, especially ones so highly skilled in the arts as these two are, that is."

"Li Si Shin, who trained the first ranks of Ravenhawk scouts in combat warfare, nearly a thousand winters ago… it was said that he spoke often of the Shinobi and the shade warriors, and passed down what he knew of their arts. The little I know of them comes only through the training scrolls we have today that he left behind. I never imagined they would appear in Attera, let alone in the middle of the Stonewood Forest, working with Marghans," Joshen explained.

"This is a strange mystery," spoke Lurandor.

"Well, it is one I am certain we will find goes deeper and is stranger than we can fathom, as more parts of this mystery are revealed to us," replied Joshen. "We must also tell Master Southern Pheasant Li about the appearance of these shade warriors, as soon as we are back in Arden. I'm sure he will find this information to be of great interest and importance. Maybe he can then shed more light to give us deeper insight as to what their appearance might fully mean."

"Ravenhawk Scout Chief Bo Fan Li's mother was a master in the Iga Shinobi style of the ninja arts from the land of Go. She passed all she knew on to him. The Shinobi and the demon sorcerers of the Kage No Senshi, the shade warriors, are both ninja clans and are juxtaposing factions that have been in conflict with each other in a vast but secret war throughout Jin Go Mei for several ages. We need to seek him on this matter as well!" spoke Lurandor.

"Speaking of Bo Fan Li, let me tell you of Kharvack's message from the Scout Chief. Kharvack said that Silverwood was attacked by a group of Marghans and a jingrol. We know this is the same group of mongrels we just vanquished. Lurandor, it has been ages since any Marghan raiding party has attacked something as large as the Silverwood Village."

"Yes indeed," agreed Lurandor.

"Bo Fan Li said this was two nights ago. They reached Silverwood Village the morning following the assault. After his Ravenhawk scouting party investigated the attack, many interesting facts that didn't add up presented themselves. Bo Fan Li knew we were in the area and sent his black hawk bird to tell Kharvack what happened so that Kharvack could swiftly get the news to us. He had searched since then and only found us now."

"So what strange facts were found?" asked Lurandor, wanting Joshen to get to the point. Curiosity was a weakness of Lurandor, but this situation would have piqued anyone's interest.

"Well, the village guards weren't killed by traditional Marghan weapons. Tiny, almost invisible and nearly undetectable, dart marks were found on the bodies. Someone was covering their tracks and removed the darts. The nature of the marks reveals that they were from a highly skilled professional. They had hit vital areas with pin-point accuracy. All twenty of the night watch guards were killed the same way that night inside the village walls. There was one particular building and it was the Priests of Maltos Study Shrine. All the teachers, scribes and sages were knocked out from some type of spell or…" Joshen paused.

Lurandor answered, "Knocked out by Koji gas commonly used by shade warriors."

"Yes," replied Joshen.

"The rest of the village was attacked by the destruction of flames from the jingrol's fire belches and the carnage reeked by the Margahns. As you already have concluded the obvious I'm sure, the Margahns and jingrols were just a distraction and a cover," Joshen explained.

"Yes, I have and do agree wholeheartedly. The Marghans would never risk something that big. They prefer smaller targets they can easily handle. The shade warriors were using the Marghans and jingrols to cover their movements and aid in their plans," spoke Joshen.

"What plans I wonder?" Lurandor asked as he mulled over Joshen's words.

"They were obviously not looking for loot or plunder at Silverwood. They were looking for someone or something, and it seems tied to the Priests of Maltos Study Shrine since it was attacked differently and not by destructive means."

"Looks as though they wanted to capture someone or something alive."

"That was my conclusion also," Joshen concurred.

"What would someone want from them?" Lurandor thought out loud.

"I don't know if Bo Fan Li knows or has figured out that shade warriors were involved yet. Bo Fan Li and his team are staying there in Silverwood helping deal with the safety and damages of the village for the time being."

"Are there no Sages of Nivari there to help as well?" Lurandor asked.

"There were a few monk sages there and a scholar sage I believe. Kharvack reported they were all killed in the night during their sleep by the assassins before the main raid," answered Joshen. "Also, something peculiar caught my interest concerning the Silverwood attack. The Nivari Temple was completely destroyed while the Maltos Study Shrine suffered no damage in the slightest."

"So again, we must conclude and concede to the fact that they must have been looking for someone or something at the Priests of Maltos Study Shrine," Lurandor repeated as he seemed to fall into deep thought.

"So there is the first mystery: what were they looking for?" Joshen asked.

"A wicked riddle indeed," agreed Lurandor.

"Figuring out this mystery will be like chasing a rabbit through the brush in the dark with a hunting hound with no nose," Joshen shook his head as he said a well-known Mejian cliché.

"I feel we will be chasing this rabbit down a hole for a while, and we shall need to pray he doesn't find a back door before we can grab on to him," Lurandor replied using another old Mejian cliché.

"My friend, I fear this rabbit has many holes and has dug them deep. I fear we will be hard-pressed to dig a near bottomless hole before we find the rock bottom truth of what is and has happened," replied Joshen.

"I at least have already caught and captured the rabbit's tail and have it for you to see as a key clue to understanding the riddle in front of us."

Joshen spoke as he reached into his pouch while Lurandor watched him with anticipation. Bren, now much calmer, even looked up in curiosity. Joshen's hand stopped in his pouch. He kept it there and got up looking around as if someone in the forest may see them.

"I found this among the equipment and gear on the shade warrior I disposed of."

He walked over, stood between Lurandor and Bren, pulled his hand out of his pouch and opened it. A stone, the size of a large eagle's egg, lay in his palm. When the sunlight hit it, colors swirled within it. It looked as if liquid light swam and mixed inside it as if it had a life of its own.

Lurandor gasped, "Ya-El! What can this be?"

Lurandor's face illuminated as he looked at the stone.

"I take it you may know what this is," Joshen spoke.

"I feel a strong essence radiating from it. It is the same essence I feel from the spirit of Ya-El that falls on me when I pray. Though evil men were carrying it, there is no evil spirit or power about it," Lurandor explained as he looked at the stone.

"I have a strong inclination this stone wasn't made here on Attera. I have heard many tales, legends and songs passed down through my people," he hesitated as he looked at the stone again. "Light moves within the stone; it looks as if it has a life of its own.

"Yarval, an Ilbri elder of my people, was said to have made many wondrous things in our home world of Hollinedan. I cannot be sure but I believe this is… well, my best guess," the Ilbri paused with his eyes still lit up. "An Auram! By the light of Ya-El!" Lurandor gasped.

Bren had never seen the Ilbri showing this much amazement or emotion regarding any particular thing before.

"What's an Auram?" Bren asked as his curiosity overtook him, giving him a burst of strength and energy to speak even in his current weakened and shaken emotional state.

"It just may be one of the light stones created by Yarval," replied Lurandor, still with a stunned tone in his voice.

Lurandor and Joshen who both had their attention wrapped up completely in the strange stone didn't seem to notice Bren had asked a question.

"But how? As far as I know one of the light stones of Yarval was used in creating the Celestial Radiance Portal, the bridge that the Ilbri used to travel from Hollinedan to Attera. I do not know how many Auram were created or if he brought any with him from our home world when the survivors arrived in Attera as they fled through the Celestial Radiance Portal. To the best of my knowledge, the Auram or the light stones have never been seen in Attera.

"So we may have more than one rabbit to chase at a time. If it is truly an Auram, how can one be here and how did these shades get their hands on it?" Lurandor asked as much to himself as to Joshen.

"I feel the energy from it; it feels like the same emanating from the…" Joshen paused to look and see if all around them was clear from any possible evil ears.

"We should not talk about it here, but I have felt the same anointing and power from something else as well."

"Yes! Put it away quickly!" Lurandor exclaimed. "I think we need to now make some serious but hasty decisions."

Joshen put the stone back in his pouch.

"The rabbit hole is deep and mysterious indeed," remarked Lurandor, still in awe.

"There are only a few still living in Attera that could possibly give us an answer to solve the mysteries of the stone. The Grand Sage Ruebal Enok the Zanari, and Muirwen and Lanos, Queen and King of the Ilbri, who have some of the oldest living memories in Attera. Muirwen and Lanos have walked in both worlds and were the ones who lead the survivors from our dying world to our new home here on Attera many ages ago. In fact, they alone are the last survivors of the original first refugees."

"We need to get this stone to Cedar Ridge as fast as possible," Lurandor said.

Joshen nodded in agreement. "Whatever this stone may turn out to be, I feel it is a matter better kept between us. I feel there are many spies now, even among the ranks of the Ravenhawks, more so in the past few winters since we have been allowing non-Mejians to join us and become Ravenhawk scouts."

Joshen continued, "The shade warrior ran because he didn't want to risk combat or get caught. I believe the sole reason was he was trying to keep us from finding this strange stone. It was obviously of great value and importance to him."

"Joshen, what do you think is our best course of action?"

"I believe we should keep the knowledge of both the shade warriors and the mysterious stone to ourselves; less chances to reach enemy ears. We must, with all haste, get the stone and news back to Cedarwoods and call the Elders of Arden together and alert them to what has happened here. We must then send word to Yar Samaya to the Ilbri Elders, Muirwen and Lanos. Now here is the last bit of new and recent information that must certainly be revealed to you, Lurandor. But I feel Kharvack should reveal it to you since this last piece of the puzzle comes directly from a recent dangerous encounter he had. After hearing his tale you will see why I decided to save the worst part of the news for last."

Bren, who had been listening while fumbling with his gear again, now raised his head once more in full attention so he wouldn't miss one word from Kharvack's tale.

Kharvack cawed and cackled seemingly to clear his throat as he stretched out his large black feathered wings. The large black hawk bird was making a big show of himself now that he was the center of attention. He seldom got to tell stories or talk about things other than give the messages he relayed for Joshen to other scouts or messenger birds. He was basking in his moment.

"Craww krae cacaw!"

"Kharvack!" Joshen interrupted the bird. "You need to calm down and relax. I don't believe you realize you're speaking in your native blackhawk bird tongue which only I, among us here, speak, and I have already heard your tale. Please speak in the common tongue of Attera so the rest of us can hear your story."

In his excitement, Kharvack had forgotten the minor, but important, detail to speak in common Atterian. Lurandor was chuckling to himself. He thought the bird and the old scout would make a good comedy jester team that could perform and make a good living working for one of the traveling Mejian shows.

"Sorry," cackled Kharvack.

"I was flying from Silverwood... caw cack caw... and was making my way here to find Joshen with news from Captain Bo Fan... Caw kuh caw, and on the way I found this rather fat mouse that was stuck in a hole in an old oak tree. I had to fly closer to get a look. He was squirming and my stomach was squirming from hunger. I thought it nice of Ya-El to provide me with such a fine breakfast that I didn't even need to work to catch. Caw ki caw... I guess the mouse had eaten too many nuts and couldn't fit back down his little door hole and had gotten stuck. So I decided..."

"Kharvack!" yelled Joshen. This time Joshen had a hot tempered tone in his voice.

"I don't think Lurandor or Bren care to hear about a fat mouse and a small hole and about what you had or didn't have for breakfast. Though filling your stomach may be important to you, there are more pressing matters that we must discuss and deal with this day. All three suns are high in the Atterian sky and before the moons start to fill it, please tell us what we need to hear."

Again Lurandor held back his laughter. As usual, the two provided him with great entertainment and had done so on a regular basis.

Kharvack flapped his wings ignoring the scout's scolding words and proceeded to tell his tale again.

"After I finished my breakfast, I flew straight for this area, caw caw keh caw. And I saw circling in the sky above the tree tops some odd shaped flying creature. I first thought it was an eagle that had caught a snake or a rooster that was bitten by a snake and was now flying while the snake still held on. But as I got closer, I saw it wasn't any of those things at all. Caw caw. It was a flying mongrel. It was a creature that was half snake and half rooster."

It was Lurandor who interrupted Kharvack this time, but for another purpose than to keep the bird focused. He looked toward Bren as he spoke. Lurandor, being one of Bren's mentors, always made use of any situation that may be beneficial to Bren's education.

"Bren, do you know what these creatures are?"

Bren paused a second and then answered, "I think I know."

"I read about them in the book Tinkmut carries around with him, Tinkmut's Gazetteer and Encyclopedia of Attera. In it, I remember reading once that there is a creature called a 'roosnake'*, I believe. I think they were part of the mongrel monsters that Ipolus created. They were made when he mixed the flesh of a snake with a rooster creating a mongrel monster."

Bren paused as if recollecting and then spoke again, "Aren't they used by the enemy as messengers and assassins?"

"Yes," replied Joshen. "You are correct. They are highly dangerous and venomous mongrels."

Joshen then turned and spoke to the large black bird, "Kharvack, now finish your story."

The large bird, undaunted by the interruptions to his story, started his tale up again.

"As I flew near, kaw kaw, I realized this was some unnatural mongrel. I, myself, had first heard about them from my grandfather who claimed he saw a roosnake way back many winters ago. Of my flights all across Attera, this was the first one I have ever seen. Kaw kaw ka kaw. I noticed it was circling above the tree line as if it was preparing to catch some prey on the ground.

"It didn't notice me as it was too intent on looking at what was on the ground below it. I decided to fly closer, and as I got closer, I was then able to see through the forest tree tops to the ground. The roosnake was circling right above where I saw Joshen going through the gear of a man dressed in black who appeared limp and dead. I saw as Joshen pulled a stone from off of the man in black, at nearly the same moment the roosnake looked as if he was getting ready to take a dive at Chief Joshen. I went into a dive myself and took advantage while the mongrel was focused on Joshen. I dove through the air as fast as I could and grabbed his serpent tail. I then turned using the momentum from the fast speed of my dive, and I threw him through the air, kekaw kaw, like a giant whip. I then followed him as he was flung through the air and grabbed him with my talons before he could recover. I drove them deep into his back. The roosnake screeched in pain. His long neck turned and struck at me, and I had to swat it with a wing and let go of my grip to keep from

A Roosnake

getting bitten. The fang bite just barely missed me."

"My feathered friend, if you had been bitten just once, you would have been dead before you finished falling from the sky," spoke Lurandor.

"Poisonous! Caw caw yes! Kharvack knows this!" acknowledged the bird.

"After the roosnake was free from my grip, he was hurt and he took off through the air heading east. I chased him for a short while. As I pursued him, I heard other screeches coming to join him in the sky, and at a great distance, I saw more than a few dozen roosnakes flying towards the one I chased to join with him. I turned back and flew as fast as I could to return to where I found Joshen. They didn't seem to follow me. Kharvack did good? Kaw kaw."

"Yes, you did," Lurandor praised him. "Your fast thinking, like Bren's today, saved Joshen's life."

"He is now I guess indebted to you I'm sure," Lurandor added this while looking to see Joshen's response. He knew he was in a friendly way provoking the old Ravenhawk.

"Ya-El blessed you with great timing in your return but you could have easily been killed Kharvack," Joshen chided. "Roosnakes are extremely dangerous and deadly foes."

This answer was the closest thing of a "thank you" he would get from Joshen.

"You're welcome," cawed Kharvack.

Joshen, ignoring the bird's usual sarcasm, quickly spoke, "We haven't seen roosnakes in these numbers anywhere in Attera for ages. They serve only their Sarn and Nephal masters. Their return no doubt marks the return of Ipolus," Joshen wiped sweat from his brow and looked up to the sky as he spoke.

"That is for certain," agreed Lurandor and then added in a serious tone, "The return of roosnakes in great number flying in the open skies in the light of day means only one thing: Ipolus is now on the move and is ready to bring another all-out war in his conquest of Attera."

Joshen firmly spoke with a stern tone, "Now we clearly see the enemy's servants on the move and no doubt doing so under his orders and command. After many ages of working behind the scenes and directing from behind a veiling stage curtain, Ipolus has now prepared himself in secrecy all this time. It seems that he has done so mistakenly too soon, by openly showing a small part of his face revealing his presence just before he steps back on center stage. This return to moving more openly in Attera for whatever evil purposes, I fear, he has been long planning.

"He has worked for so long biding his time in the shadows unseen; I believe whatever Ipolus has planned for Attera, he is initiating it now. I fear he is ready for his revenge upon the good folk of Attera. We must now at least consider the grim fact the enemy will now know we have killed two of their shade agents and have in our possession this mysterious stone. These roosnakes that Kharvack saw, I'm sure have already flown over most of Kayna, carrying the word of what has happened here to probably almost every enemy servant in every direction around us," Joshen looked towards his companions and crossed his hands in front of his chest as he spoke. Lurandor noted that his old friend did this every time he really meant serious business.

"Today we were hunters. I feel like now we shall soon be the ones hunted," Lurandor stated.

"All the more reason we must take no excess time in getting to Cedar Ridge Cottage. While we are here on the far western side of Kayna, we will find few allies to help us. I fear we have to deal with many dark agents of the enemy before we can reach Northern Arden and to the home of the Zanari Sage Ruebal Enok, and without a doubt, he will in haste send messengers out to call a meeting for the Elders Assembly of Arden to come meet together in council once again," Joshen asserted.

"Kharvack," spoke Joshen, looking directly at the bird.

"You must fly south from here towards Suthnia and seek Captain Keffa and his squad. He was leading a group of Ravenhawk scouts to Suthnia on a mission. He may be there still or heading back from there traveling northbound towards us on the Allowin River Road. They may be the only help we can find in this part of Attera. Tell him it is urgent to meet with us as soon as possible. We will more than likely be on our way to Gormall Bridge."

"Kaw, yes, kawkaw!" squawked Kharvack.

With that, the bird took off. Before Kharvack could fly too far, Joshen was yelling at him to return.

"Kharvack! I'm not through with you! You must listen to me. Do not engage the roosnakes! Avoid them at all costs. Flee the moment you spot them."

"So you do care about Kharvack then?" the bird butted in.

"If you are killed, we will be cut off from communicating with our allies. Keep yourself alive!" Joshen strongly cautioned.

"Thank you for your concern for Kharvack... Kaw kaw," the bird took off not allowing Joshen to get in another word, giving himself the last word or so he thought.

"Warn the other Ravenhawk messenger birds about the danger of the roosnakes!" yelled Joshen.

Kharvack cawed and squawked as he flew out of sight.

"May be time for a new messenger bird" is what Lurandor heard Joshen mumble from under his breath as the bird flew away. Lurandor shook his head and smiled trying not to laugh. Joshen had little to no patience when dealing with the blackhawk messenger birds. Lurandor always enjoyed the raw entertain-

> **Tinkmut's Gazetteer and Encyclopedia of Attera**
>
> THE KINGDOMS, TOWNS, & VILLAGES OF ATTERA
>
> *Excerpt, added and written by Robnob Haborav - Woodland Gnome and Scholar Sage*
>
> THE KINGDOM OF MEJIA: MUELLAN VALLEY—
> The Muellan Valley is located between the Eastern Erez Mountains in the Kingdom of Mejia. Many Ilbri settled there to live among the forests as close neighbors to the Mejian people. Three thousand years ago, when they arrived in the world of Attera from passing through the Celestial Radiance Portal from Hollinedan, they brought with them various types of seeds from their home world and planted them all throughout the valley of Muellan. From these seeds many trees, plants, flowers, fruits and vegetables grew that over time spread all over the valley. The Mejian people who ate the food grown from these other-worldly seeds increased their life spans from around 150 to 500 years and this trait carried on to all their offspring. The Atterian animals that ate these plants native of Hollinedan grew in size and their senses, abilities, strength and intelligence were greatly magnified. In some cases, they even began to change into nearly new kinds of animals. The large Muellan deer, the favorite steeds of the Mejian people, are an example of this.

ment he experienced when he got to see Joshen deal with the eccentric birds.

"Bren, Lurandor and I shall dispose of the bodies of the shade warriors so they will not be found. Go and gather our gear and get our Muellan* deer ready to ride."

Bren, now somewhat calm, got up and ran to the edge of the meadow, grabbed a rope, and pulled their hidden gear down from the top of a tree. As he let the gear reach the ground, he pulled a small horn from his pack. Made from a ram's horn, he blew it. The sound echoed through the forest. Within minutes, three large Muellan deer came running with great speed through the woods to stop at his side.

"Neena, Larma, Pello. I see you have missed me!"

The large Muellan deer all seemed to affectionately nuzzle Bren at once. Bren gave them each in turn an affectionate pat before he packed the gear and fixed their saddles.

"Pello, mount," said Bren.

Pello ducked his head and lowered to his knees, allowing Bren to climb onto his back. Bren rode Pello, with Neena and Larma following, into the center of the meadow to wait for Joshen and Lurandor.

Chapter 6
NIGHT VISIONS

Bren didn't have to wait long, in just a few moments Joshen and Lurandor were seen walking through the tall grass towards him.

"I see you've got our Muellan deer gathered, packed and ready to go," said Joshen, as he and Lurandor walked towards their respective Muellan deer to prepare to mount them.

"Yes, Sir!" replied Bren.

"Tighten your cloaks and tie up your gear and strap it down. We are in for a fast hard ride," Joshen cautioned them.

"Shall we head straight east through the Stonewood Forest until we hit the Allowin River Road?"* asked Lurandor.

"Yes, there we will follow it south to the Gormall Bridge and cross into the mostly woodland realm of the Kingdom of Kayna. Traveling straight through Hillock's Valle, following the old Gormall Trail from Skeanville to Hallenthorpe, it's about four to five days travel if we keep a good steady pace. That course as best as I can figure would be the safest and most time efficient route we could take on our way to Cedar Ridge. The dense tree lines that flank the trail will be good cover for us in case we have any roosnakes that are trying to track our movements from the air. I'm sure any and all servants of the Dark Enslaver that the roosnakes could have reached by now, are all alerted and on the lookout for us," Joshen explained.

"Yes. If Ipolus is behind this as we are almost certain, then we can count on the fact that every spy and mongrel from Amara to Sarnia will be searching for us, marking our trails and paths, especially because of this strange stone we have taken from the shade warriors. As I have said before, I feel it is of great importance to our enemy. I have a tingling sense that as we learn more and investigate deeper into this mystery, this stone is a key component to the grand scheme the Enslaver has planned," remarked Lurandor, as he began adjusting his boots getting ready for the coming ride.

"We are on top of the enemy's most wanted list again it seems," Joshen spoke as a small smile came across his lips.

"Joshen, I don't believe we have ever not been on top of his list since we first started adventuring together ages ago."

"We must take honor in knowing that the most powerful force of evil known to Attera or the late world of Hollinedan knows our names quite well. As they

Tinkmut's Gazetteer and Encyclopedia of Attera

GEOGRAPHICAL & DEMOGRAPHICAL ATLAS OF ATTERA

Excerpt, added and written by Robnob Haborav - Woodland Gnome and Scholar Sage

THE ALLOWIN RIVER ROAD – The Allowin River Road follows the course of the Allowin River on its Western side, from where its name is derived. The road runs near straight north and south starting in The Kingdom of Amara at the Gates Road of the City of Kelvinstad running all the way down to the Kingdom of Suthnia. For the most part, it runs mainly through and along Amara's Eastern Southern Border while Kayna's Western most border lies just across the river. The Allowin River Road is the second largest and busiest trade road next to the East Oriental Spice Road. It stays in constant use year round, full of merchant caravans and travelers.

say in Mejia the land of your people: 'You have won no valor, nor can call yourself any kind of hero until your enemy knows your name and speaks it more times a day than your closest friend.'"

"It will be like old times my friend, which come to think of it have been pretty much the same as the new times, we quest… we do missions… we almost die…we complete our mission just in time to start a new one. You know, our only vacations have been traveling from one mission to another. I guess I should have found us missions from locations farther apart, so I could at least have better stretch of a vacation," Lurandor laughed.

"Ipolus and his minions do not rest, so how could I ever rest?" Joshen answered. "Though if I may speak with candor, I am… getting too old. No matter what I may tell myself, it's a fact… that my body will not be able to keep the same pace as the old days and maybe I've already ran past the finish line that destiny had already laid out for me. I was thinking that maybe it was time to retire but after what we just found out…" Joshen paused as if in thought. "I guess I will not be able to experience that quiet retirement, and that peaceful permanent vacation from the Ravenhawks now."

"You don't sound too convincing that you are in any way disappointed by your tone," pointed out Lurandor with a smile.

Joshen ignored the Ilbri's keen observation, proving to Lurandor he hit the mark, and continued speaking again quickly changing the subject.

"So yes, those roosnakes by now have informed anyone in league with the shade warriors what has transpired here. I fear many servants of the Dark One will be on the lookout for us, if not already hunting for us," replied Joshen, almost sighing, as he seemed to be thinking out loud. Lurandor noticed that his old friend seemed to be repeating himself and appeared to be stretched out thin and stressed, at least more so than usual, even for Joshen.

"Agreed, so we need to plan well carefully choosing each path, trail or road before we take it, making sure we avoid the enemy's snares, spies and hunters, as we did before long ago when we were the hunters chasing his servants through wild lands and kingdom alike!" Lurandor answered. He was purposely speaking with a lively tone as his intention was to pull Joshen from his inner thoughts. "The quicker we get this strange stone to the Grand Sage Ruebal Enok, the better. Time I fear will not be on our side. After all these long years have passed, so many seasons after the Sarn Wars, and now in this very age, we will see the Dark One rise again from the shadows attempting to enslave all of Attera."

Joshen didn't reply but nodded his head and gave a grim look. He expressed the deep heartfelt words as he gazed towards the heavens, "May Ya-el give strength to us and to all the good folk who have the courage to stand against the coming darkness."

He then sighed a loud breath, looked directly towards Lurandor and proceeded to speak again, "My friend, we have seen many, many years full of scores of Ravenhawk missions. My aged and somewhat working memory recalls these scouting assignments often, as I look back down the stretch of time from days long past. I see and relive in my mind often an uncountable amount of battles fighting his servants, some of which we only survived due to nothing short of divine intervention. We have been diligent in our duty serving Attera, and I began to believe that it may not happen, before my spirit walks the celestial winds. I feel that fate may have a sense of humorous irony; now after all this time, we see signs of Ipolus and his full reappearance. I must be honestly forthcoming and speak my heart in hopes I may remove some of the weight from pressing on top of it. I must confess, Lurandor, that I am frustrated this is all happening in my later years when my body has seen too many adventures, and it now seems no matter how fast I continued to be on the go pushing myself forward, age has outran my pace and caught up with me. Now that the best of my fighting is behind me, I fear our biggest fight is in front of me. In the twilight of my years, the real war of our age is just dawning."

"I know Ya-El has his purpose; all in his timing," Joshen shook his head and smiled finding faith in the irony of the situation.

"Every rain drop and flower petal has its destined place to rest on the ground and its given time to fall; there is purpose, time and reason for everything under the three suns," quoted Lurandor from a well-known verse from the sacred text of the Scrolls of Illumination.

Lurandor and Joshen both felt the urge that they needed to be off and not tarry any longer; the three mounted their steeds and turned their Muellan deer rides to face east. With a word of command from Joshen, their mounts in response, all sped off at once. The strong antlered steeds carried them at speeds greater than any of the fastest horses of the Eight Kingdoms could reach. The three riders went straight into the tree line entering the thick woods at the far side of the meadow. The powerful Muellan deer penetrated through the dense branches and ground foliage, not slowing down in the slightest or even missing a step. Where horses could not take their rider, the tall deer from Mejia drove forward at a lightning pace. Their great agility enabled them to find a trail through places where no path seemed to exist.

Bren, still not used to riding the massively large Muellan deer, held on tightly to the stirrups, hugging his mount around the neck, looking over Pello's head and through his great antlers seeing Lurandor and Joshen riding just a few paces ahead.

Bren looked to the side; tree trunk, branch and leaf blurred by him as Pello followed Neena and Larma while they agilely raced through the woods. Leaping over log, stone and stream, the three made their way through parts of the forest that even a veteran adventurer's horse would find difficult to navigate at a walking pace. The Muellan deer had been used for nearly three thousand winters, as mounts for travel, battle and hunting by Bren and Joshen's ancestors, the sons of Leban Mejia. It was truly a well-known fact in the Eight Kingdoms that no mount in Attera can match them trekking through forest, hill, or valley. These remarkable mounts simply took their riders with great unparalleled speed on any terrain.

As they speedily went through heavily wooded areas, Bren, even while holding on for what he thought was the sake of keeping his life, was able to notice more stone monoliths that were spaced randomly through the forest and wondered again where they came from. From time to time, he noticed moss and vine-covered stone and brick work that were part of some ancient large, unidentifiable structures. As a result of erosion and decay, the vine and moss made them look more part of the dense forest itself than the remains of some lost civilization. He wished they had time to stop and explore some of these crumbling ruins. He had a keen love for history and such things, and as they passed many clusters of ancient buildings, crumbling pillars, and lone vine covered stone arches, he wondered who had built them all and what kind of people might have dwelt there many ages ago. The young Mejian boy felt like the forest had an old deep sense of something ancient; he sensed a presence emanating from it that made him feel like he was traveling through an ageless time.

Suddenly ahead, the three riders came upon the remains of a thick, nine-foot high stone wall. Bren nervously noticed the Muellan deer charging straight ahead towards the ancient stone barrier did not slow down at all.

"Hold on!" Lurandor yelled back to Bren.

At this point if Bren held on any tighter, he would be choking Pello.

Bren watched as Joshen and then Lurandor riding on the backs of their Muellan deer went leaping, flying over the wall, clearing it by several feet. He took a deep breath and held it as he saw the wall swiftly approach while opening one eye to peer ahead through the antlers of his mount. He felt Pello tense and kick off from the ground, leaping high into the air at full speed. He closed both his eyes and didn't open them until he felt his mount hit the ground running with a grunt and a snarl on the other side of the high stone wall. Pello then raced forward, on the heels of Lurandor's mount.

As the sun started to set in the west, Joshen and Lurandor slowed down their mounts to a steady trot. Pello imitated the other deer's pace, pulling in close behind them.

"We must be very near the Allowin Road now," observed Joshen. "I don't want to camp any closer to the road than this. We shall wait till morning to travel on the road."

What would have taken anyone not traveling by Muellan deer two days' journey, the three travelers had made it to the edge of the Allowin Road in half a day.

Lurandor leapt off his mount and scaled a nearby tree as fast as any squirrel could. In just a few moments later, he was yelling down at his companions from somewhere at the top of it.

"I see a dense line of trees running north and south several miles ahead. Those must be the same ones that follow the border of the Allowin River Road." Lurandor's Ilbri eyes were as keen as an eagle's even in the dim twilight of evening.

"Good. We can set up camp here among these thick hickories. The forest is dense here and will cover us well enough to light a fire," Joshen said while he was already unpacking gear from his mount.

As dusk settled, Joshen lit a fire as they finished setting up camp. Lurandor opened a traveling pouch that was part of the scouting gear that was strapped to his Muellan deer and pulled out a tightly wrapped package and unraveled its contents.

"Here," offered Lurandor as he handed Joshen some dried fruit and berries and baked flat bread. To Bren he did the same. He then sat down and joined them.

"I didn't realize how hungry I was until now. I just realized we haven't eaten in more than a day. Back at home, I don't think Reyva ever allowed me to even miss so much as one meal or any snacks in between she thought I was due to have," Bren said.

Joshen smiled, "Such is the life of a Ravenhawk scout; a rewarding path to follow but a very hard one to keep following."

Bren didn't make another comment; filling his empty stomach became the only priority of his actions and clouded any other part of his thoughts. He could not believe how much better his food tasted after not having eaten for so long.

After they satisfied their hunger and rested, Joshen rose and pulled out a wooden whistle from one of his inner pockets to see if Kharvack was in the area. Joshen blew his whistle; no sound came forth but the sound of air. The tone of the whistle was set to a pitch that only the large Ravenhawk birds could hear.

"Now we shall see if he is close. The old bird should be heading back from Gormall Bridge I hope, with word from Captain Keffa. That is, if he can stop chasing fat rodents for dinner."

Weary and tired, Joshen then stretched out on his worn travel blanket. Bren was already wrapping up in his, lying on a pillow he made out of his Ravenhawk cloak.

"Sleep well friends. I'll keep watch tonight." Lurandor said this as he had noticed for some time now, how tired and weary Joshen looked.

"No arguments," Lurandor spoke firmly while staring at his intended verbal target, Joshen. Before Joshen could get a word out in protest, he added quickly, "I need to use this night to meditate and pray." Of course it wasn't just an excuse intended by Lurandor to get Joshen to go to bed and receive some much needed rest; he truly felt he needed a good night of refreshing prayer and meditation to reinvigorate himself.

Lurandor spoke to his companions in a tone that showed he wouldn't take any other options. He wanted his friends to fully relax and rest. Ilbri need very little sleep, and as long as they are meditating regularly, they can go for days without it, with little signs of weariness.

With that, Lurandor scaled up a nearby tree. Joshen was already fading into sleep. Years ago, a much younger Joshen would have fought to take first watch and do his share. Lurandor noticed a slight change in his friend that had been slowly creeping up on him in the past few days. Deep down he knew that age was catching up to the old Ravenhawk scout. Just in recent years though, Lurandor realized that he had been worrying more and more for his old friend.

Joshen looked to be in his mid fifties, but looks and age are deceiving when it concerns Mejians.

Mejians live much longer than other races of men. From the time their ancestors planted and started to eat the food grown from the seeds that the Ilbri had brought from Hollinedan, their home world, the life spans of the Mejians went from one hundred to five hundred years within one generation.

"Joshen has to be in his early five-hundreds," Lurandor contemplated to himself about his dearest friend.

Bren tossed and turned most of the night. Every time he closed his eyes, he saw scenes from the skirmish they had fought in, running through his mind over and over. The visual images of his first battle were burned forever in his young mind. They were playing themselves out in his thoughts and emotions. As to be expected, his first battle had stolen from him some of the naïve perceptions that he had about the world and the Ravenhawk lifestyle.

Robnob, his guardian and mentor, had often told him as a piece of advice something along these lines, as Bren heard the gnome's voice in his head, "Real experiences, and in most cases, the trying and dangerous ones, are what mold a person into who they are and who they become. At times, it's only the things that cause and leave scars that have enough power and strength to change us. Every piece of wisdom has its price; pain is often the price of growing into a mature person. You will learn at times pain is the only currency that can afford or be used to purchase wisdom. It usually never comes for free."

Feeling overwhelmed while being overly reflective, Bren wondered how much his first battle had actually changed him. As he lay with his travel blanket wrapped around him, his mind pondered and dwelt on thoughts that certainly no child his age should ever have to internally deal with. Eventually as stressful thoughts usually do, they made his mind weary. It was then that he first felt the real extent of how exhausted he truly was. Having been pushed hard in recent days and by the experience of recent events, Bren's physical body was shutting down forcing him to rest against the inner will of his mind. His body and heart still felt tension resulting from the stress from the recent circumstances of his first battle. Emotions of excitement mixed with fear strongly pulsed inwardly, burning in his stomach like fire through dry bush. After many hours of staring into the dying embers of the campfire, he eventually dozed off into an uneasy sleep.

It has long been said by the Zanari Sages that until the long awaited day that the hammer of justice falls, the Shedim* shall wander freely throughout the lands without ever ceasing; tirelessly they roam to and fro. They seek who they may devour and destroy. That is the dark way of the twisted entities, consumed by cruel hatred and darkness called the Shedim, the demon spirits of the dead offspring of Ipolus spawned from the mixing of his seed, an act forbidden by the All-Creator Ya-El. Their unrelenting mischievous missions they gladly do with loathing animosity, pursuing with vile intent those in the light, those who still have physical bodies and a soul. Their tireless effort goes on without ceasing for a moment, seeking to plague and torment the living mortals, the good folk of Attera, who are the children of Ya-El. The night is their playground; from shadow to dark shades, they travel seeking poor beings, upon whom they may direct their malicious hatred. Once the three suns disappear over the western horizon and the twin moons appear heralding the darkness of the night, this is the time when sleep falls upon most of the free folk throughout the Eight Kingdoms. It is also the time when the Shedim peak in their evil activities. When slumber consumes a being, their conscious awareness enters another reality, another realm, and becomes significantly more vulnerable. In the sleep state, the mind cannot guard and protect the thoughts of the heart and soul with the same clarity and strength as when fully awake and sober. This is how the Shedim prefer their victims to be, more helpless and considerably more vulnerable. Wickedly all the forces of Ipolus rejoice in preying on the weak and downtrodden. They revel in dominating and assaulting those who cannot put up any resistance or fight back.

Worn out and troubled, Bren lay in an uneasy sleep that lacked any form of peace allowing him to receive very little true rest. While staying in a troubled slumber, sometime late in the night, Bren had a horrible dream of men in black outfits creeping out of the woods coming towards their camp. As they moved

Tinkmut's Gazetteer and Encyclopedia of Attera

ENTITIES & BEINGS OF THE CELESTIAL REALMS

Excerpt, added and written by Robnob Haborav - Woodland Gnome and Scholar Sage

SHEDIM—The Shedim are known as the dark demon spirits and foul phantoms. "Shedim" is the proper name for the countless disembodied souls who are doomed to walk in the shadows of Attera without the housing of corporeal flesh and blood until Attera sees its last day, the final forging of Ya-El will commence, and the foundations of the Eretz (world) will be broken, undone and made new. In that day He will hammer out and sift all souls, separating from the good folk of Attera all the creatures, beings, spirits or entities who had chosen to walk down an ancient evil path following their master, Ipolus the Enslaver, into the oblivion of chaos and destruction. As a blacksmith forges and hammers the impurities out of the raw metal ores so shall Ya-El cleanse all of Attera.

Origin of the Shedim

When Ipolus mixed his seed, doing what was blasphemous and forbidden, with beast and women folk of Attera, the Sarn and Nephal beings were born from this evil union. Ipolus' father was a fallen Iryn (celestial watcher/ messenger of Ya-El) which made him part celestial and part terrestrial. Ipolus' evil offspring who are born of female beings of the terrestrial realm (physical material world) mixed with his seed which is part celestial (spiritual cosmic universe), are called Sarns (Ipolus' seed mixed with beasts) and Nephals (his seed mixed with human, Ilbri, or gnome). When these beings die or are killed, their souls which are torn between realms are not allowed to walk the celestial winds to see the throne of the All-Creator Ya-El. They are doomed to roam Attera as dark shadowy demons, seeking to enter and possess any physical body they can access. These demon spirits are called the Shedim.

forward from the shadows they had been lurking in, they began slowly getting closer with each passing moment as they moved towards Bren. He was gripped tightly by the crushing talons of panic; all he wanted was to flee. Bren attempted to get up, he found himself paralyzed, unable move any part of his body at all. He felt as if an unseen weight pressed down upon his entire body not allowing him to move or even speak. As the ominous black figures came very close, they appeared they were preparing to strike. Bren felt horrible fear and an unnatural anxious sensation grasp his entire being. He tried with all his might to yell but he couldn't get his lips to even move to get one sound out. Unable to move, he felt so horribly powerless, terrified, and completely vulnerable. As the dark shadows neared him, what he felt in that short cluster of moments, from his perceived viewpoint, appeared to last for days, though in reality only a small span of time had actually gone by. In times later as many seasons passed, when Bren found himself looking back attempting to grasp on to this particular memory to retell what happened to him this night, he found he could never fully describe it with mortal words. He felt that no words in any language could do justice to the amount of evil and hatred he felt had emanated from all around him, and how terrifying it was that most of the dark presences that he sensed that night he knew deep down, were focused solely on him.

 Bren was startled and surprised when suddenly coming into view, a hand from one of the dark shadowy figures appeared in front of his face reaching for him. He thought with great certainty that his heart would stop as he tried to cry out in terror for help but only soundless air blew from his lungs as he lay paralyzed in the same manner he would have if a dark warlock had turned him into a statue of cold stone with a wicked spell. The long black fingers were inches away from touching him when suddenly, from what seemed to be coming directly from out of the starry sky above him, Bren heard a clear and melodic voice singing. The sound fell upon him, hitting him briskly with the same potency as the caress of sunlight would on bare skin when it first reaches you, emanating through the cool morning mist as it brings forth a fine spring day.

 Immediately he awoke from his horrible dream and sat straight up, well more like jerked straight up, as sweat dripped from his brow and stung his eyes. He was trembling, feeling truly shaken from the dream. He turned his head and looked to see Joshen lying on the other side of the fire, breathing in a slow rhythm as he rested in a deep sleep. He shook his head and rubbed his eyes as he wondered briefly if he was still dreaming or if he was awake. He still heard the singing as he continued to shake the sleep from his eyes. Then as he became more awake, he realized the song and voice he had heard in his dream that drove away the dark sinister hand had come from Lurandor who was still singing from his high perch hidden somewhere in the treetops above their camp. He looked up through the boughs in the tree that stood directly above where he had lain. In the dim illumination from their campfire, there was little chance that he could hope to see him. He then lay back down and listened.

Seeing Joshen near him and hearing Lurandor's voice relaxed Bren and allowed him to feel as much peace as a twelve-year-old boy could experience under the circumstances and after having such a horrible dream that had felt all too real. He couldn't understand the language of the Ilbri in which Lurandor was singing. Lurandor's voice was soft and melodic and had a beautiful flowing quality to it. Despite the fact Bren couldn't make out the words, the melody moved him and captured his emotions and thoughts as it slowly seeped deep into him touching him to the core.

The music of Lurandor's voice caused Bren to relax and his body grew less and less tense as the Ilbri's vocal melody poured over him the same way the early morning sun would dispense into a meadow as it broke above the horizon removing the coolness of night and the chill of the early dew. Before he knew it, he was once again deep into sleep. As his body slept, his mind was awakened and he began to have a dream.

It was more of a guided vision than a random dream that Bren experienced that night, though he knew it not. He became aware and conscious in the dream and what his eyes first

remembered seeing was the view he saw as he was floating, flying as light as the breeze that had been blowing across and over the forest where they camped. The sun had risen and the sounds of a forest stream flowing through the woods filled his ears. He heard leaves being rustled by a gentle gust of air and it blended in the manner of an orchestra with the noise of songbirds chanting, echoing through distant trees. He saw everything through the hue of colors he had never experienced looking at before and everything was more clear and beautiful than he had ever seen before anywhere in the waking hours of his life. It was as if he was seeing a different world that was both fantastic and amazing and yet it was still as familiar as Attera for him. Lurandor's melodic song had caused and penetrated his dream and now seemed to lead it. The music took shape as a light that shone as a faint, soft radiance on Bren's mind and took form as sunshine rolling over a meadow full of golden flowers. Bren hadn't realized it but stress was fleeing from him, as he experienced a warm rush of peace flow over him and wrap around him as a wool blanket would. The shackles of fear fell from him.

Lurandor's song changed melody and it also caused a corresponding change in Bren's dream. He found that he was taken to another place, another realm, another world. He was dreaming of cities full of Ilbri shining with splendor and glory. He flew over high towers shimmering with large stones that sparkled like constellations in deep blue hues. Countless palaces and many gardens full of fruits and bloom filled the landscape. He witnessed a host of beautifully strange animals and songbirds, the likes of which he had never observed before in Attera. Bren also saw many strong and magnificent griffins flying through white clouds in a bright blue sky. There was a strange large bird that flew also in the sky. It was shining in bright red and gold plumage and its tail feathers were long and danced on the winds as it soared across the sky, flickering like flames reflecting the light of the brightest day Bren had ever seen. He felt as if he was catching a long glimpse of a timeless place lost in the antiquity of ancient days found only now in the form of story and song.

On a flowered hill, he saw a large stone pavilion surrounded by large white columns with statues of griffins on them all facing toward the center. As he looked up at the sky, he could see stars flickering and shining. Bren saw something strange as he looked at the stars whose pattern was not the same as he knew and was familiar with on Attera. Then as if someone was drawing with lines of blue light, these lines began to connect the stars that he saw. As a result of the drawing of these lines of light, eight constellations became distinguishable for him that lined up stretching across the sky. Suddenly a group of stars that were unseen before appeared and burned brightly. A new constellation was now visible while the stars from the other eight constellations disappeared. Then its stars grew dim and went out. After a few moments, the stars of the new constellation reappeared and became brighter until its radiance out shined making dim all the other stars with their constellations. Bren right away knew the stars were in the pattern of a giant bird with a long tail. For some strange reason, he knew this constellation was the same large multicolored bird he had seen earlier in his dream. It was a bird he had never seen before anywhere in Attera in person or in one of Tinkmut's many books on the creatures found in the lands of the Eight Kingdoms. Bren then looked down from the sky and looked at the pavilion again. He saw in its center was a beautiful great sword whose blade seemed to be made out of some glowing blue metal that looked opaque like a gem. It was in the hands of a crumbling statue of a warrior. This statue stood in a large fountain of water that had blue flames that seemed to burn from the water like an oil burning lamp. He saw a man with golden hair walk towards the fountain. He was dressed in all white robes trimmed in green and blue. He grabbed the sword and held it up towards the sky and spoke in the Ilbri tongue, "May the light of Ya-El forever shine upon us and may the darkness forever flee from it." For some unexplained strange reason, Bren understood what he had spoken.

Bren noticed the Ilbri had a gold crown on his head. On both sides of the crown were two bright golden forms of griffins. Their eyes were made from the same substance as the sword and they began to glow as the sword in his hand did. In the center of his crown was set a golden gem that was as radiant as the sun, and on both sides of it were two smaller gems that were also made from the same opaque blue stone. The two gems came to life radiating light.

Beside him an Ilbri woman with dark raven hair came to stand. She was so pretty Bren could never find the proper words to do adequately describe her beauty when later attempting to describe the dream to someone else. She wore a crown of three woven chords that were metallic and reflected light. The chords' hues were blue, yellow and green. She had a large vase in her hand and she dipped it into the fountain to scoop up some of the water that resided there that had blue and white flames that danced above its surface. She held it up and spoke words in the Ilbri tongue, "May the water of life burn forever with your presence and may your sacred flame Ya-El burn in the hearts of our people for now and until the end of all days and beyond." Again Bren for some reason could understand her words in the Ilbri tongue.

The whole pavilion shook then and the entire surrounding environment started to quake. Two of the great columns fell and the statues on top shattered as they hit the stonework flooring on the ground. The two Ilbri turned and ran down a flight of stairs that were connected to the pavilion. Soon the whole area around where Bren was standing in the dream was shaking more and more violently. He heard a multitude of voices screaming at once from every direction around him.

He looked down from the pavilion and saw mountains spewing forth red flame and smoke and he watched as burning lava began to consume great cites in the distance. The ground opened up and swallowed the great city that lay in a large valley before the pavilion. A huge black ominous cloud came towards him, and as soon as the smoke and ash reached him, everything went black.

His dream then changed suddenly. He found himself transported to another place. He was standing inside a great large hall. He looked up and saw the hall's center had a great glass dome located in the middle of the ceiling through which sunlight shone. He saw the golden sun in the center of the sky and then two other smaller orbs of light that were glowing, one with red and one with blue light. The two orbs both moved and stopped as they lined up directly in front of the sun. There was a light flash that burst as a result that filled the sky. The three objects in the sky had joined and become one and their illuminated colors mixed creating a beautiful violet light that changed the color of the sky. The sky now with its purple hue revealed stars that made up eight constellations which looked like those he had seen earlier in his dream and the ninth larger one in the shape of the large, mysterious bird appeared with them.

As he looked down from the ceiling, he noticed in the center of the hall was a large round fountain similar to the one he saw previously in the dream. The fountain stonework was made of smooth ivory-colored stones. In the center of this fountain was a huge olive tree that seemed ancient and mysterious. As the violet light fell upon the olive tree, it bloomed with gorgeous blossoms and large green olives grew forth. But the tree quickly aged and started to turn dark and wilt. Bren then saw that the fountain had no water in it.

From a door in the hall came a young beautiful girl that he had never seen before. She had long golden hair but her face looked like she was a Mejian. She walked in and poured from a vase she was holding and again he saw the blue flame water. It poured from the pitcher and filled the fountain. As the water reached the roots of the tree, it sprang back to life and grew and was flourishing once again, sprouting bigger and more beautiful, and its top grew and broke the glass as its upper branches rose and grew towards the sky.

The girl then began to sing in an unknown language and with a voice whose dynamic volume filled the room. It was more beautiful than anything he had ever heard. When she sang, the olives on the tree became ripe and began to glow with bright light. The leaves of the tree glowed as well and they also changed in what they were made of. They looked as if they themselves had turned into pure light. Then suddenly he looked up and across the room, his eyes focused upon a crumbling statue of a warrior holding the same blue sword as the one he saw in the great city earlier in his dream.

The statue appeared to be ancient and showed signs of severe erosion and as

Bren stared upon it, the large stone figurine began to move. It walked into the fountain and the blue flames from the water surrounded the crumbling statue. The warrior statue held the sword up and then the blue flames rose from the fountain and wrapped around the entire statue and the sword. As the flames receded, he perceived that the statue was no longer of decaying stone, but that it took flesh and became a man. Before he could see the man's face, the man turned into a large bird wrapped in flames. This was the same unidentified bird in the constellation. The bird held the sword in its claws and flew through the dome in the sky. Bren suddenly saw a large, black serpent-like Drukos Wyrm* that flew through the sky. Its shadow brought darkness and malevolence with it that Bren in that instant felt chilled to the bone. The large bird went flying straight towards it. Before the two met in the sky, he woke up suddenly and abruptly.

It was Joshen's voice that snapped him out of it. Bren at first immediately wanted to tell his mentors the dream. It seemed so real and life-like. But he quickly realized that he had overslept and his companions were in a hurry to hit the trails forward and there was no time for them to waste hearing his dream no matter how odd and spectacular he thought it was.

"Rise and awake, the light from the morning's first sun Mesham already caresses all of Western Attera," spoke Joshen to his young apprentice. "We need to be on our way before Tashat and Asha join Mesham to fill the sky!"

Bren rubbed the sleep from his eyes and felt a little worn out in body, but strangely he seemed rested in his mind and heart. His spirit felt cleansed and refreshed, and the horrors of the battle from yesterday now seemed like a distant cloudy memory. He knew that it must be the direct result of Lurandor's song. There seemed to be an inner power that came from it. Bren shook himself from his deeper thoughts. He couldn't keep from thinking about the dream and that was when he noticed Joshen was already almost done finishing up packing his camp gear.

"I can't always be lagging behind making everyone wait on me," thought Bren as he rushed to get his gear packed on his Muellan deer. As he was packing he saw Joshen blowing the silent whistle used to call their messenger bird to them.

"Kharvack may be in the area now. Let's wait a few minutes here," said Joshen.

Lurandor again ran up the side of the tree with ease.

"I'll check our surroundings before we go," Lurandor said as he made his way to the top of the tree.

Joshen finished packing his gear and preparing his Muellan deer for another ride. As soon as he was done, he turned and quietly without a word, walked away from the camp towards a dense portion of the forest disappearing into the heavily wooded nearby tree line that surrounded the clearing they were in. Bren had just finished packing up his gear on Pello when he looked up and saw

Tinkmut's Gazetteer and Encyclopedia of Attera

THE CHILDREN OF IPOLUS: SARNS, NEPHALS & MONGRELS

Excerpt, added and written by Robnob Haborav - Woodland Gnome and Scholar Sage

DRUKOS WYRMS (OR, SARN DRAGONS) – **Race: Sarn.** The Drukos Wyrms are the offspring born from the blasphemous works of Ipolus the Enslaver. He mixed his seed with dragon females creating this new race of Sarn creatures. The Drukos are much larger and extremely more powerful than the dragons they were born from. They are free will beings and have the ability to speak languages. They are vile creatures and are all together evil and wicked, serving their father Ipolus. They have the ability to speak and breathe fire that comes out and burns with the power and strength of flaming red scorch-water. Fighting for their master and father Ipolus, the Drukos Wyrms destroyed and devastated much in the Eight Kingdoms of Attera during the Sarn Wars. They were proven to be nearly unstoppable. It was the joint efforts of the flying griffons and giant iron back turtles, both native folk from Hollinedan, that were able to defeat and destroy the Sarn Dragons almost down to extinction. They are now rarely seen anywhere in Attera. They enjoy eating farm animals and flocks and farmers when the opportunity arises. They are obsessed with treasure and wealth.

Joshen leave. Right away Bren was curious. Joshen always in the past had kept good communication with his companions and never left or parted company with Bren or Lurandor without notifying them on where he was going, why he was doing so and when he would be back. Bren felt that he shouldn't follow Joshen but his curious nature was far stronger and more in control of the decision making part of his mind than his sense of caution and reservation. Bren as quietly and with as much stealth that he could move forward in, followed Joshen. He stopped after a few minutes of quietly trekking after his mentor when he saw Joshen standing a short distance in front of him facing the other way, all he could see was the old Ravenhawk Chief's backside. Joshen appeared to be looking down at a small running brook that stood just in front of him. Bren stayed back and out of sight, hiding among the surrounding tree trunks, leaves and forest foliage as best he could to make sure that the keenly perceptive Joshen would not see or notice that he was there in case he abruptly turned his head around.

Joshen stood there as still as a stone statue for a few moments by the small forest stream. As Bren watched his mentor intently, he heard the morning song birds sing, as leaves rustled overhead, being disturbed by a cool spring breeze that was making almost as much sound as the running water in the brook made, as it went gushing and flowing around rock and stone, perpetually traveling on its way to distant places.

Slowly Joshen reached into his travel cloak and pulled out a large white flower that Bren at once recognized as a lily. Joshen then, very methodically, raised it to his lips and kissed the flower and whispered some words too quiet for Bren to hear from the distance of where he was hiding. Joshen cast the beautiful white lily into the brook and it was carried away by water. As the water's current took the flower downstream, Joshen, to Bren's complete surprise, started to sing. He had heard Joshen on only brief special occasions sing in the past. The melody was ancient and its flow was deep and moody and it all too well matched the tone and sound of Joshen's low and boisterous voice. The song instantly struck Bren hard piercing to the core of his heart as he felt the emotion and power behind Joshen's singing. What the old Mejian Chieftain melodically cantered was beautiful but it had no sense or even a trace of cheer or rejoicing to it. The overwhelming ambiance it had resonated unmistakably as sorrow. Bren felt sad though he did not know why or what the song was about; it made him feel as if his heart would die in his chest. What moved in him made him think that it was he that felt loss and yearning as he listened and had no idea why these particular emotions flooded and overwhelmed him. The melody of the bittersweet song he heard that morning never departed from his memory; it had easily left a lasting impression on him. Joshen sang in a more ancient dialect of spoken Mejian that was now little used among his people except by the oldest living elders. Here is his song as Bren later remembered hearing it translated into the common speech used in Attera.

> *Fade too soon the flowers in the grass*
> *Withering in moments that do not last*
> *Comes the morning with no warning*
> *Seeing the sun for the last time glisten in the early dew*
> *Hiding in crumbling towers from the past*
> *Memories tumbling showers of the only Lass*
> *Who sweetly said hi then forever said goodbye*
> *Missing the caress of hands from the only Love I ever knew*
>
> *Gone too soon,*
> *Under sun or moon,*
> *I shall hear her voice no more*
> *Beyond time and space*
> *I must walk the winds to that place,*
> *To embrace again the flower, I adore*

  Bren quickly left his hiding spot and headed back to where their camp was as soon as Joshen had stopped singing. He had no idea as to what the song meant or why Joshen, in a ritualistic manner, cast a lily into the running brook. He was now overly curious wondering what all of it really meant.

  Reaching the clearing where their mounts were, Bren right away went to his Muellan deer Pello and started fumbling around with his packed gear making sure to give the appearance he had been busily doing so the whole time Joshen was gone. Whatever Joshen had done, Bren knew it was sacred to his mentor and seemed very personal. The last thing he wanted was for Joshen to find out he had spied on him while he was doing something that had appeared to be very private and special. Regardless of what it actually was that Joshen had done, Bren especially didn't want Joshen to think he was being rude by not respecting Joshen's privacy. He had great respect for his mentor and didn't want Joshen to lose any respect he had for him.

Moments after Bren started his rouse of re-adjusting gear atop his mount, Joshen came strolling through the tree line into the clearing. Bren was relieved and very glad when he saw that Joshen had showed no signs in his mannerisms or expressions that he had caught Bren or knew he had followed him.

"Has the 4th day of the month of the bear sneaked its way upon us already? Each winter seems to come faster than the one before or so it appears to those who have seen too many seasons as we have," spoke Lurandor as he projected his voice down the tree he was in towards Joshen on the ground below him.

Joshen just nodded slightly in recognition of Lurandor's words and then proceeded to go straight about his business. Bren began to wonder why the 4th day of the month of the bear had any significance and what was the purpose for Lurandor to specifically mention it. Bren concluded and decided that it must be associated with what Joshen had done earlier by the brook, since he knew of no festivals or observances associated on that calendar day practiced by the Mejians or anyone from any other race or folk in the Kingdom of Arden.

"It looks as if the surrounding forest seems quiet and nothing out of the ordinary seems to be happening. Not much going on except a black object with wings I now see in the far distance, flying straight for us," yelled Lurandor again from the top of a tree.

PEOPLE OF ATTERA

Lurandor Hollintree

Joshen Reza

Bren Reza

Made in the USA
Middletown, DE
18 March 2017